Diamondcrabs and Mangoes

Interstellar Spring Book 2

J. Darris Mitchell

Other Books by J. Darris Mitchell

Interstellar Spring

Fireflies and Cosmos

Iceoaks and Warblers*

The Wild Lands

The Legend of the Wild Man

*to be released in 2017

This book represents hours and hours of work done by the author as well as many other people he both loves and respects. Don't steal it. If you are interested in sharing it, contact the author and he will be happy to assist you. It violates the sacred bond of writer and reader to reproduce or reprint any part of this book without the author's written permission except for brief quotations in critical reviews. In other words, reprinting or reproducing this book is illegal. It's totally OK to let a friend read this copy, but please direct them to the website so they can purchase the rest of the series themselves and thus help the author and those that he loves and respects put food on their tables.

Thank you.

This is a work of fiction. All of the characters, events, and organizations are either imagined by the author or used fictitiously.

INTERSTELLAR SPRING: *Diamondcrabs and Mangoes*

Copyright 2017 by J. Darris Mitchell
Version 2.1
All rights reserved

Cover Art by Sam Mayle
Find more at https://sammaylearts.myportfolio.com/

Independently Published
ISBN 9781521206300

For my sweet Raquel,

I wrote this while you fed our baby

I hope your dreams were sweet as nectar

Contents

1

The metal pipe rattled and shook, and, like something out of the Wild West, thick, black sludge erupted from the ground. The group of organic engineers cheered. It was the third find they'd had this month, and if the analysis of the crude oil-like compound was anything similar to the last few underground seas they'd discovered, it represented billions of credits once refined and traded to the other Seeded Worlds. Juxor would continue to grow wealthy off of the natural carbon resources it possessed just beneath its surface, as would the men who came to this planet to help develop that resource.

'The priest will be happy,' one man dressed in coveralls stained black with the tarry sludge said as he twisted a gasket and slowed the gush of carbon slurry to a trickle.

'Oh I already am, and outside of the worship ceremonies on the seventh day I am not a priest, just a faithful servant of the Organic Church, and your planetary marine biologist.'

'Yes, Mr. Kane,' the worker said, smiling bashfully like a kid who was caught saying bad words and not reprimanded as harshly as he'd expected.

'How is it looking, Dr. Kirk?' Kane asked.

Roberth Kirk approached the hologram of Kane. His white lab coat had far less grime than the coveralls of the laborer. He consulted a tablet connected to a vial of the black, carbon-rich sludge. 'Very good, sir. Purity rivaling the old fossil fuel deposits of Earth-1. This is the best we've found on land.'

'It's as the Doctrine says, those who search will find what they are searching for,' Kane said.

'Mother Ocean provides,' a good number of the men in grungy coveralls muttered, an affirmation of their faith. Dr. Kirk frowned at the men.

'We need to get this cleaned up, Mr. Kane. If Dr. McKenna's hypothesis is correct we have very little time. A lighting storm is approaching.'

The holo of Mr. Kane laughed. When he did, the workers laughed with him. 'Osha's hypothesis, if you can call it that, has been proven correct only a handful of times, and has been flat out wrong dozens more. Besides, *Doctor*, you are hundreds of meters inland. You should be quite safe from any oceanic alien bugs, if I recall what Osha named them.'

The men laughed at that. Again, Dr. Kirk frowned.

'That will be all, Doctor. Now, leave the devoted to their work.'

'I have room for more,' Dr. Kirk said to the group of men.

Some of them looked at the hologram of Kane, but no one stepped forward.

'You have your beliefs. We have ours,' the man who'd spoken earlier said. Some of the men behind him nodded. Dr. Kirk sighed, climbed into a drone, and took flight.

From there, the perspective of the holo shifted to the camera mounted underneath the drone. It lifted up to see that the men, the carbon-sludge well, and the machinery were on a small island, and that to the horizon was nothing but ocean broken up here and there by other islands, most of which were bare and rocky, though a few supported tufts of green. The sky was a thunderhead thicker than anything ever seen on Earth-1. Bolts of energy cracked from the sky to the sea. The drone started to fly off towards the east when the Doctor started to curse.

'Back down! Down!' he yelled and hammered something on a keyboard.

Over the ridge of a sandy dune on the small island scuttled a wave of creatures.

'Enhance,' Captain Catalina Solaris Xao Mondragon said, and the holo obliged. It zoomed in on one of the creatures. It had a craggy exoskeleton, four legs, and two arms tipped with shimmering, dark, metallic-looking claws it waved menacingly. It was hard to tell their size, bigger than a man's hand certainly.

'The report says they're made of diamond—the claws are anyway.'

Captain Mondragon nodded. 'Proceed.'

The crab-like creatures poured over the sand dune and made for the machinery slick with the carbon slurry. The men didn't hesitate. One of them had a tool that sprayed a liquid on the crabs. There was a spark from the tip of the machine, and then the creatures were burning. They did not stop, but only added a high-pitched squeal to their unwavering march towards the men.

'Get on!' Doctor Kirk yelled, but the holo of Kane spoke louder to the men.

9

'If we lose this reserve their population could multiply. Stop them now.'

The men reached for their weapons. Some of them had projectiles that were illegal to transport through interstellar space. Others simply had sharpened pieces of metal. They attacked the crab creatures with mirthless determination as wave after wave scuttled past and onto the machinery that had found the organic sludge.

Their claws made short work of the metals and carbon composites that made up the machines. In moments, the pump was a pile of scrap and the black sludge was again pouring out of the ground. The crabs soaked their claws in it, then brought it to what must have been their mouths. Satiated, some began to excrete a black filament as others shuttled them around. All the while thousands more of the creatures poured out of the sea and over the dunes. The men's attempts to slow the tide of crabs made no impact in their numbers.

'Stop the flame thrower!' Kane yelled. The man wielding it turned off the gout of flame and for a moment the crabs coming at him paused. One of them waved a claw at its compatriots. A dozen other crabs waved back. Hundreds more mimicked these crabs. They all stopped going for the organic sludge and turned on the man. Then they eviscerated him. Their claws tore him into a thousand little pieces. Where one moment was a man the next was nothing but a pile of meat. The crabs gobbled it up greedily. Some of the crabs began to eat the sludge from the man's coveralls and excrete long, thin, black threads. One of them turned and waved to the thousands of other crabs. Thousands of crabs waved their claws back and did the odd little dance. Then the thousands of crabs attacked the workers.

'Oh Darwin, do we have to watch anymore?' First Officer and Interstellar Botanist Farah Relkor said.

Captain Mondragon paused the video. 'No, I suppose we don't.'

'What happens from there?' Fin asked. Fin was the pilot of the *Artemis*, and thus would be the only member of the Organic space ship that wouldn't have to go down to the surface of Juxor to face the creatures.

'The crabs kill the rest of the crew, eat them, and then the holo goes dead due to an electrical storm. The report says the storm lasted for days and was too strong to risk any kind of reconnaissance. When it was done, the contents of the well were gone. All that was left was a mass of that thread, carbon pellets that they assume are excrement, and bits of the diamond shells. I have specs on that loaded on all of your tablets.'

'This is strange, Sola, and potentially dangerous. I don't think you should go down; it might hurt your perfect figure and surely that carbon sludge would not agree with your sense of tidiness. No creature like this was included on the seedpods, and records don't show any ecologists releasing any crustaceans recently. I don't see how a crab with diamond claws could evolve from a mollusk in the 75 years since Juxor was seeded. It's not even remotely like any insect I know. It had no wing stubs, nor did we include any aquatic insects in the seedpods during the Great Seeding. More perplexing are the diamond claws. Still, this holo leaves me with one big question,' said Roman Jupiter, the entomologist of the *Artemis* and ex-boyfriend of Captain Mondragon.

'If someone introduced it illicitly?' Ikamon, Farah's husband and the ship's Interstellar Marine Biologist, said.

'Possible, I guess,' Farah said, 'but who would be dumb enough to introduce a non-sanctioned species on a planet as important to trade as Juxor? I mean, anyone with the clearance to transport enough specimens to establish a viable breeding population ought to know better.'

11

'What was your question, Jupiter?' Fin asked.

Captain Mondragon, Farah Relkor, and Ikamon turned to Roman.

'Who is Osha McKenna?'

2

'Typical. Gotta get the woman, you chauvinist slug,' Farah Relkor said, her caramel skin going dark with anger as she sliced a tomato furiously. Despite her slender, almost bony frame, Catalina never doubted the fury of her First officer. On any other ship but the *Artemis* she probably wouldn't have been promoted, but Farah was too good of a botanist for Catalina to be bothered by a bit of crude language. Even now, her dark green and yellow uniform was covered in grass stains even though they'd been in space traveling under the faster than light Bubbledrive for days. She'd probably earned the stains harvesting the vegetables she'd grown aboard the *Artemis* for their salad.

'Farah, please calm down. It is not healthy to be so angry, you know?' Ikamon, Farah's husband, said. Ikamon was currently preparing the main course for dinner, clams he'd harvested from the oceans of Wholhom and let multiply aboard the *Artemis* in one of his massive aquariums. He wore an apron over his green uniform that, unlike Farah's, was clean. He was the opposite of his wife in so many ways. She was dark skinned, he was pale, Farah's straight blonde hair was usually unkempt or tied back lazily to be free from her eyes, while Ikamon's was always styled down to the follicle. And best of all, when

Farah was furious, Ikamon was cool-headed. 'Please try a clam. They are very delicious.'

'I will have you know that, much like the caterpillar of the monarch butterfly, I am attracted to one flower only, and that is our beautiful captain.' Roman grinned at Catalina over his fresh-baked cricket croutons. Catalina ignored him. They'd dated back when they'd all been crew on the *RL Carson* together, back before Catalina was the most decorated captain to fly a ship for the Institute, back before Roman had forgotten her and definitely before he'd fallen in love with her again. She still found his wide grin and strong nose attractive, and she loved how he filled out his uniform. Ecologists could look a little dumpy wearing the green jumpsuits that were standard fare for the scientists that worked for the Institute for Organic Expansion maintaining living conditions for people on the 51 Seeded Worlds, but Catalina had to admit that Roman always made his look great. He wore the sleeves rolled up so his big, muscular forearms stuck out, and the front zipped low so his hairy, burly chest begged Catalina's eyes downward. His brown hair was always disheveled despite his clean haircuts. Catalina found that somehow refreshing compared to Farah's complete lack of interest in doing anything with her hair or Ikamon's obsession with it. Not that Catalina wanted anything to do with Roman that didn't directly support their work in upholding the Charter. Not anymore. Roman Jupiter continued, 'I only ask about Osha McKenna because it sounds like she has a theory about these things, and theories about this bizarre behavior is something I am currently deficient in. My intentions are professional, and I am certain that, compared to our captain, she is but a cricket compared to a katydid.'

'Deficient, I like that. Can we put that on his uniform?' Farah sneered.

14

'Enough, Officer Relkor,' Captain Mondragon said, standing up straighter and adjusting her uniform. Despite her diminutive height, Catalina commanded respect when in uniform. She knew people found her intimidating. While most Interstellar Ecologists struggled to look presentable in their baggy jumpsuits, Catalina was the image of perfection. It fit her ample breasts and curvy hips as if the cut off the uniform had been made specifically for her, and as far as the Institute was concerned, it might have been. There was no officer more decorated than Captain Catalina Solaris Xao Mondragon. As captain, she had saved over a dozen worlds and millions of lives from manufactured ecosystems gone awry. It was said that there was no threat to the Charter that Captain Mondragon could not solve. Catalina believed that respect began with appearances, and controlled every centimeter of hers. Her curly, full-bodied hair was always kept under control in a tight, clinical bun. The seventeen badges of honor she wore on her breast were perfectly straight. Her uniform had not a crease or a wrinkle. Her boots shone like the stars and her gloves would find no dust if dragged across any surface of the *Artemis*, well, save her crew's labs. Despite how much Catalina prized her appearance, she valued quality work far more, and was willing to allow her crew's appearance to be less immaculate than hers, if only because she respected them enough to know that she could find no one to replace them. It didn't help that she had known Farah and her husband for years before Catalina had become a captain, and had slept with Roman more times than she could count.

The only member of their tiny crew that wasn't like family to Catalina was Fin, and the young, plucky pilot was already ingratiating herself to Catalina like a niece she'd never wanted. She was short, though still taller than

Catalina, a little plump, had close-cropped pink hair, and piercings that seemed to come and go. She wore the top half of her grease-stained uniform unzipped and tied around her waist to expose her collection of punk T-shirts made from hemp grown across the Seeded Worlds. She was currently wearing one that said 'Astro-bitch' and had a blurry image of someone playing a guitar. Catalina would have forced the girl to dress better, but they were days away from any other human contact, and besides, Fin had insisted on running maintenance on the ship as well as flying it. A pilot as skilled as Fin was rare; one that could fly and fix was practically mythical. Better to keep the girl's uniform clean for visitors, rather than get it dirty from scrubbing algae filters.

'I was wondering about that though, Captain,' Jupiter said, his grin far too wide. 'Has the Institute commended our work on Wholhom? I thought you said you'd put in a good word for me so I could get my hands on those,' he pointed at Catalina's chest.

'Compost him!' Farah said, standing up from her seat in the cafeteria, nearly flipping her plate.

'What?' Roman said innocently. 'I was pointing at her badges!'

'Seeing as how the Institute wants you back on Earth-1 for deserting the *RL Carson* a year ago, I don't think they're much in the mood to bestow you with honors,' Catalina said.

'Captain, I support your decision to go to Juxor, you know? But is it not true that are we going against Institute orders by not taking Jupiter to the…ah, cesspool that is Earth-1?' Ikamon said.

'Yes and no,' Catalina said, spearing a mouthful of lettuce and one of Roman's cricket flour croutons. She'd already finished her clams. 'I decided to take this mission to Juxor because it's closer to Epsilon-V. I hope that when we finish on Juxor perhaps we will be able to unravel what is becoming of that mission we were forced to abandon. I believe Ensign Jupiter will be instrumental in shedding some light on those monsters that killed Dr. Mercurian.'

'I doubt it. He was a far better entomologist than you ever were, Jupiter,' Farah said.

Roman shrugged. 'Eh, I haven't been eaten by cockroaches. I say we call it a tie.'

'You are beyond disrespectful!' Farah said.

'Why must you both fight? Here, drink. The clams are best with beer. Roman, your croutons pair very nicely with Farah's salad,' Ikamon said, pouring both Roman and Farah more strong beer.

Even after knowing Farah for years, Catalina had no idea if alcohol would help or hurt her temperament.

'When Fin first spotted the message, we were on shaky ground. A code orange is serious, but now that we've seen the organisms are taking human lives, we can operate under the assumption that this is a code red,' Catalina said diplomatically.

'There's never been a code red like this, though,' Fin said.

'Bugs have never killed before, so there's been no reason to put it in the book,' Roman said.

'Not until Epsilon-V they hadn't. I'm beginning to wonder if the Institute hasn't sent us back to Epsilon-V precisely because of that. A member of our crew died there. Dr. Patrick Mercurian was the first member of the Institute to ever be lost to the organisms that aid mankind's survival amongst the stars. We will solve this horrible problem, show the Institute the importance of our work and the competence of our crew when dealing with an unknown threat, and hopefully earn Ensign Jupiter the right to stay aboard, under a probationary ranking if necessary. When they see how we solve the problems facing Juxor, I trust they will send us to Epsilon-V to face the bugs that killed Patrick.'

'And hope that they've developed a taste for entomologists,' Farah said.

'Captain Sola, I can't help but notice that Officer Relkor is directing most of her admittedly inferior and juvenile humor at me. Like a rhinoceros beetle in a rain storm, I will attempt to endure this barrage of ultimately benign assaults, yet I feel that perhaps, if I wish to truly express myself, I will have to speak with you later on, in your quarters, privately.'

'Normally if you had any problems with this crew, I would say put them in your log, but seeing as you are under orders to go to Earth-1 for trial, I suggest you start writing about how much you missed your time aboard a vessel upholding the Charter and how you can't understand why you ever left,' Catalina said, hoping to cut Roman's come-ons short.

'What I don't understand is why I ever left you,' Roman said. Catalina caught his smoldering eyes and cursed to herself as she looked away. Even just a glimpse of those brown beauties, so full of desire for her, and she'd slip. Catalina had been through his lover boy crap before, and was not going to fall for it again, especially this close to a planet with an organism that was eating people.

'How can you deal with this crap?' Farah hissed while Fin fell into a giggling fit.

'Loyalty to a captain is not to be underestimated. But, Jupiter, I will not be honoring your request to council unless perhaps you busy yourself helping Fin clean our algae vats, as it seems our pilot is done with her meal.'

'Of course, Captain,' Fin said, straightening up and trying to recover from her giggling fit. 'Dump your bug biscuits in the composter, Jupiter. Let's go clean the air scrubbers.'

3

The flight to Juxor had Kensei 'Ikamon' Mizuyama pondering his place aboard the *Artemis*. One of the reasons he'd signed up to work for the Institute for Organic Expansion was because he'd watched the oceans of Earth-1 overfished to nothing. By the time Kensei had been old enough to go fishing on his own, the seas had little in them save jellyfish big enough to sink ships, and the detritus they fed on. Gone were the whales, gone were the dolphins, gone were the tuna and salmon and hundreds of other fish his grandmother assured him were special treats when she was a girl, and that the people of Earth-1 actually ate regularly when *her* grandmother was a child. It was almost unbelievable to think an entire planet's ecosystem could have crashed in just a few generations, but climate change and unchecked pollution had proved as disastrous as any asteroid. The extinctions only took slightly longer, though the fossil record would notice no difference between a few years and a few decades.

Ikamon chose his name and decided to join the Institute when he went to his first holo-aquarium. In it, he discovered a projection of a giant squid armed with ten tentacles, octopuses strong enough to drown a man, and oysters—delicious, faceless creatures that still managed to clean the oceans far more efficiently than the machines the corporations swore would save the people of Earth-1 from their own filth. Kensei saw something of himself in those creatures. A man of the deep who cared for little besides eating and traveling the yawning abyss. He styled himself Ikamon that day, "Squid-man" and stopped responding to his given name, "Mizuyama," which meant "Water-mountain." A nonsensical name for a person who didn't exist anymore. He'd signed up to work for the Institute in hopes of seeing these creatures that only existed on Earth-1 as holograms or frozen DNA sequences, and, if Darwin willed it, to one day taste them. That was why he'd joined the Institute, and how he'd escaped Earth-1 and his family, but not why he'd stayed. He was an Interstellar Marine Biologist and aboard this vessel not because his interest in the sea, but for a far simpler and yet infinitely more complex reason; he stayed aboard the *Artemis* because Kensei was in love.

How lucky he had been when ten standard years later, on a failing O-Class vessel he'd been working on as a plumber, Kensei had met Farah Relkor. He had fallen in love with her immediately. She was everything his family back on the island detested. She was loud, opinionated, brash, crude, full of herself, and completely disrespectful to Kensei. She hadn't given him any time of day until luck finally gave her to him. They'd been stranded in a distant corner of Earth-4. Farah had been surveying an island to study convergent evolution, and Ikamon had wheedled his way aboard the ship under the guise that the plumbing was bad, only to discover when they landed that, indeed, the water pump off the ship hardly functioned and without it there was nothing to cool the gravgen. Kensei had assured Farah he would fix it, but while the brilliant and beautiful botanist had busied herself studying the native plants, Kensei had gone exploring and discovered a bank of dried seaweed. Wasting no opportunity, Kensei had stripped naked, swam into the ocean, and hunted until he'd found what he was looking for, a squid.

To find such a thing on an alien world was once as impossible as it presently was to find the creatures on Earth-1. When Kensei had discovered and caught the creature, he'd thanked the Institute for sending out its 51 Seedpods filled with the germs of life so many decades ago, as well as all of the men and women who'd gone to each of the 51 Seeded Worlds to survey them and introduce species they thought would bring some semblance of balance to the planets' strange ecologies. He had promised himself that if Farah would have him, he'd quit plumbing, become a marine biologist, and work for the Institute and at Farah's side for the rest of his days.

It seemed his promise would not be fulfilled, for when Farah returned from her work, tired and covered in grass stains, her dark, straight hair dusted in pollen that glowed in the red sun of Earth-4, she was furious. She had screamed at Kensei with such passion then he'd almost been overwhelmed. He hadn't been able to say a thing to her, and that was probably for the best.

For while she was completing her survey, when Kensei was supposed to be fixing the broken craft, he had prepared a meal. To his simple lunch of rice with sesame seeds he added the carefully butchered squid that he had charred ever so briefly on the fire. His grandmother had taught him that it was a grave sin to overcook meat. She had taught him that to burn the flesh of an animal was disrespectful, that each creature had a special flavor that was to be respected and enhanced. Kensei prayed to her for guidance, and hoped she could reach him from her ashes left back on Earth-1. He had placed the charred squid on the rice and rolled it up with dried seaweed he'd found. *Sushi* at its simplest.

When Farah had screamed at him, he'd said nothing, only given her the meal, poured her a bit of sake, and bowed. She'd screamed even louder at that, and for a moment Kensei feared she would flip the food he'd worked so hard to prepare into the sand, but instead, she'd started to laugh. Kensei had never heard a sound so unexpected or so sweet. He'd heard her laugh from afar and always found it intoxicating, but this was the first time her laugh was because of him. He didn't know then whether she was laughing with him, at the absurdity of preparing a meal when stranded on an island on an under-inhabited alien world, or if she'd simply found him beneath her, but he'd smiled and raised a glass and to his surprise she raised her cup, drained the sake with him, and poured him another.

They dined on the beach, on Kensei's squid and seaweed. For dessert he presented her with oysters, seasoned with nothing but the weakly salted ocean of Earth-4. Those finished, Farah smiled and asked if he had anything else for her. Kensei, still shy in the presence of this overeducated and exuberant personality, had sadly shaken his head, to which she'd laughed again and told him to close his eyes and open his mouth.

Kensei obliged, feeling himself grow hard as she scurried about in the sand beside him. How he wished she'd touch him then, but she wouldn't. She only whispered in his ears about the first colonists of Earth-4 planting mango trees and asked if he'd ever tried the fruit. He'd said no, so she had described it to him. Its flesh dripped with sweet nectar. It was supple, yet firm to the touch, and nearly melted in one's mouth. No fruit was more delicious on any of the Seeded Worlds. Farah would know, her family controlled vast agricultural fields on Earth-4. They'd probably planted these mangoes. Kensei felt his mind wandering to her body again and again. He tried to control himself, but could not. He'd feared she'd see his erection and laugh at him again, but she didn't. Instead, she'd fed him mango warm as the setting sun while he sat blindfolded. When finished, she removed the blindfold and he found she was dressed in nothing but a lacy black thong.

She ripped off his pants and laughed again before sinking onto him. Her breasts tasted like mango, her mouth like oysters. Hot and carnal. Her brown skin glowed like embers in the setting sun while her blonde hair danced in the wind like flames. Kensei thanked the universe, The Institute, his grandmother, even his corporately blinded family for setting him on the path that had led him to this one perfect moment.

He'd told her he loved her, and had for months, and she'd smiled, and told him that she knew and that maybe she'd go out with him if he got a degree and kept cooking meals for her.

Years later, Farah had somehow not left Kensei, despite him having to stay planet-side to finish his degree before he could work for the Institute. She'd been there at his graduation, with another mango that she ate seductively during the ceremony probably just to see his robes swell. He found then that he didn't care what his family or anyone else thought of him except for Farah, not anymore. His family was in the sway of the corporations then, and didn't care at all for the son who didn't want to work on building machines to purify ocean water. Kensei didn't see the point of the massive water purifiers. The machines may have been efficient filters, but they were far less delicious or beautiful than an oyster. Kensei rejected their claims of efficiency anyway; if the machines were so damn great, then why was Earth-1 so filthy?

Farah had put in a good word with the captain of an O-class ship and Kensei had become an ensign on the *John*

Muir. He found then that Farah, smart as she was, was but a low-ranking member of an amazing Interstellar organization. The Institute for Organic Expansion meant little on Earths 1-5. Each of the primary worlds of humanity had the industries of Earth-1 to assist them. Machines to clean their air, filters for their seas, hydroponics for their vegetables, and meatcaves for their protein. Thousands of colonists had introduced thousands of species of plants and animals on Earths 2 and 4 as well, so the ecological profiles there were more diverse than that of Earth-1 was. The Charter that The Institute swore to upheld meant little on those planets, but when they'd gone beyond, to the other inner worlds, worlds with fewer colonists and more open spaces dominated only by the life that the Institute had loaded upon its Seedpods, it became clear how powerful the Institute was.

Planet after planet, the *J Muir* visited, and planet after planet it saved. They introduced species of oysters to oceans for food sources, or varieties of grasses to prevent erosion and save cities from being swallowed by rivers. The captain of that ship, and old codger named Marx, was particularly partial to apples, and made a point of growing them on his ship so that each planet they'd visit would have the makings of a small orchard when the *J Muir* departed. An interstellar Johnny Appleseed, he'd called himself. Neither Farah nor Kensei got the reference.

Kensei had worked hard for the Charter all those years, eventually getting promoted to Second Officer of the *Artemis* when the First officer of the *J Muir* earned her own ship. Kensei had been honored to be chosen by Catalina Mondragon, and he'd had just one question for her, if Farah Relkor would be aboard. She'd laughed and nodded and it had been settled, and for the past year Kensei had worked tirelessly for his captain and the

Charter, but in truth he still wasn't driven like the other members of the *Artemis* were. Captain Mondragon, Farah, and even Roman to a certain extent, believed deeply in the Charter. They believed in spreading life because they thought it was the best way to help humanity, and the best thing humans could do. Kensei agreed, of course, he'd seen what would happen to the worlds oceans without a little guidance from nature's smartest organism, mankind, and he endeavored, just like the rest of the crew, to make the oceans of the worlds diverse, sustainable, and bountiful, but he didn't do it for some altruistic passion for humanity like Farah or the captain did, nor out of some deep belief in the beauty of life like what seemed to motivate Roman. Ikamon was driven by only two things, love and fear. Kensei had worked so hard studying and developing the oceans on dozens of worlds because he feared the day when he wouldn't be able to serve another perfect meal to Farah. He longed to recreate that first night on the island together, her laugh in the breeze, her mouth moist and salty with the taste of oysters, her breasts sweeter than mango juice. He'd worked for decades to bring diversity and fecundity to a fraction of the 51 Seeded Worlds because if he did, every time he returned to a planet he could serve Farah a new delicacy harvested from the sea he had fostered. Thus far, his strategy had worked well.

They'd been married years ago in a mad rush. Kensei had proposed, hoping against hope that she'd say yes to his engagement, and take him to meet the famous Relkors of Earth-4, but as usual, Farah had one-upped him. She'd said yes and demanded that Captain Marx marry them before they set foot on another planet, probably to spite her over-bearing family, Kensei realized now, but back then he was just thankful. Since then, their passion had only grown. Farah's emotions had tempered not a bit, but

26

she felt as strongly for Kensei as she always had, and Kensei knew it was in part because he had the bounty of more than a dozen worlds to woo her with.

But now, one of the oceans on a world he'd visited more than a decade ago had produced something horrible, creatures that Ikamon had never seen, but had nevertheless inherited his appetite for flesh and had turned around on their masters. Where before, Ikamon had largely been concerned with adding a bit more diversity or swelling the population of particularly delicious fish, now he had flesh-eating creatures unlike any fish or mollusk to deal with. And he knew how they'd come to be. If Farah found out, he'd lose the love of his life over something far worse than a tasty meal.

4

Even under Bubbledrive, the flight from Wholhom to Juxor took ten days. In that time, if Captain Mondragon had been strictly following orders, she could have gone to Earth-1 and left Roman Luz Jupiter there. She'd been given orders before they'd gotten to Wholhom to take the ensign to Earth-1 because he was under investigation for deserting the *RL Carson* over a year ago. The captain was supposed to take him to the Institute's offices on Earth-1 for discipline and debriefing. Catalina found this unusual. No doubt, Jupiter needed to be punished for deserting the *RL Carson*. As acting captain of that vessel and Roman's girlfriend at the time, Catalina wanted to punish Roman herself, but she hadn't heard of many instances of ensigns being taken back to the Institute's offices on Earth-1. With an experimental organic ship as special as the *Artemis,* it seemed like a waste of resources even more valuable than the time of her distinguished crew. Captain Catalina Solaris Xao Mondragon had not become the most decorated officer the Institute had ever produced by disobeying orders. It gave her no small amount of anxiety to think that by taking a code orange mission instead of following a direct order she risked some penalty to her crew. The severity and unprecedented nature of what was happening with the organisms on Juxor made her feel assured that her choice to take the formidable physical and intellectual resources of the *Artemis* to Juxor would be validated. Truly, Catalina was more concerned about the repercussions of *not* going to Juxor than disciplinary actions.

Never before had the organisms that the Institute sent to the 51 worlds a century ago killed people, and yet now it had happened twice in a standard year. Juxor was the second instance, and a far more lethal example of the organisms evolving into something dangerous to humans. The first was back on Epsilon-V, the planet Catalina had abandoned when the horrendous, giant, burrowing, insect-like creatures had overwhelmed entomologist, Dr. Patrick Mercurian and dragged his body beneath the surface. If not for the skills of her pilot, the entire crew of the *Artemis* would have been lost that day to a tidal wave of creatures far different than any organism ever encountered on any planet the Institute had surveyed in detail. And yet, for some reason, after going halfway across the inhabited sector to fetch Roman Jupiter, a gifted entomologist, who, despite being her ex-boyfriend, could prove essential to unraveling the mystery of the creatures that had taken Mercurian, the Institute demanded she escort him to Earth-1. Catalina didn't understand it. Completing their surveys on Epslion-V and unravelling how the digging bugs had evolved was far more important than disciplining Roman. Why had the Institute allowed her, their most decorated officer and captain of their most advanced O-class ship, to abandon their work on Epsilon-V to go get an entomologist skilled enough to face the threats of that world and then not let her use him to finish her work? She wondered if rumors of their relationship had gotten out, or if a new general had been promoted who had different priorities. She certainly didn't recognize General Apocrita, the man who'd told her to go to Wholhom instead of Epsilon-V, and then told her to take Roman Jupiter to Earth-1. Maybe he was to blame for the Institute's failure to recognize the dangers that awaited whoever went back to that planet. How could he be so blind to their report?

This wasn't the way it was supposed to work. It was inevitable that colonists died. It was a fact of going to an alien world that mistakes would be made, and many had argued that some of those deaths were the fault of the Institute and the organisms they'd used to seed the 51 Worlds. Especially in the early decades, it was common for the organisms of the Seeded Worlds to cause problems. Ecologists now understood that most of the planets had been explored and tampered with far too early in the evolution of their ecosystems. People saw oceans filled with green algae and an atmosphere rich in oxygen and moved in, only to face unstable boom and bust ecosystems. On some worlds trillions of flies would hatch overnight only to die before dawn, their corpses burying crops that were already struggling in the thin topsoil. The story was the same on worlds over. An organism from the seedpods would take hold on one of these fragile worlds, its population would explode, use up all its resources, then either be eaten or die from starvation. This happened for decades until natural checks and balances evolved and started to give the artificial ecosystems some stability. Some of those evolutions hurt people. There was a fly on one world that had somehow evolved the ability to suck blood, and a plant on another that had caused allergic reactions in a group of colonists so severe they'd gone into shock, but those sort of issues had happened on Earth-1, when it still had wildlife. The first generation of the Institute's Interstellar Ecologists has solved these problems as best they could, by either releasing some sort of predator for

30

the offending individual, or attempting to remove them completely, which of course proved to be virtually impossible. But that was long ago, and even in those days, the biting flies had never *killed* anyone. It was true a few children had died of anemia, but at least they'd been surrounded by their families when they'd passed instead of eaten, like the workers of Juxor had been. These days, most of Catalina's work was to ensure that the Charter that was established twenty years ago defining the rights of colonists to govern their own land was respected. So long as the colonists had breathable air, drinkable water, and tillable soil or fishable seas, they were protected under the Charter, and the planet belonged to those who lived on it. Catalina's job, and the job of every Interstellar Ecologist who worked for the Institute for Organic Expansion, was to survey the under-inhabited worlds and ascertain if colonists could live there without mechanical intervention, and if they couldn't, find a way to adjust the ecology so that the people of that world could live out on the surface as human beings instead of as cogs inside a burbdome. Typically, Interstellar Ecologists did this by establishing pollinators, inoculating farms with necessary fungi, or introducing an algae that could survive the particular salinity and composition of the planet's oceans. Nowhere in the Charter did it explicitly say the job of the ecologists of the Institute was to protect people from being eaten, but Catalina felt that to not solve this problem was to turn her back on the Charter itself.

She stood up and made her way through the *Artemis* to the bridge. To get there, she had to walk down the long, narrow corridor made of cargo vessels of the *Artemis*, that, when traveling under Bubbledrive, rode on the front of the massive ship like an arrow thrusting forward from a hunter's bow. A rainbow of colors danced under the plazzglass portholes, indicating that space was being warped from the Bubbledrive engines. Catalina owed her existence to Bubbledrive. It worked simply, so the physicists said, by shrinking the space in front of the *Artemis* and stretching the space behind the vessel. Somehow, the ship could arrive at a destination before a transmission sent from the same original location could. Scientists still couldn't explain precisely why the light danced so spectacularly when under Bubbledrive. Like so much in the world, the beautiful aurora was a mystery. Catalina marveled at it, how it had always been a part of her life. Her father told her that she had been born under Bubbledrive, and that her mother had also died under its eerie glow. Catalina found it beautiful nonetheless, a reminder of humanity's ingenuity and ability to conquer the cold nothingness that made up so much of the universe. Catalina loved to imagine the *Artemis* as it traveled through its bubble of distorted space, a cosmic bow and arrow silhouetted against a sphere of wild, artificial light. Catalina reached the end of the line of cargo crafts, walking more quietly through the vessels closest to the main bulk of the *Artemis.* She had insisted some of these cargo ships be used as crew's quarters in case there was an emergency. This way, they would all have the ability to make it to a nearby planet and, better still, Farah and Ikamon's cries of passion wouldn't travel through the walls. Catalina entered the elevator and felt a slight twinge as the artificial gravity reoriented itself to the floor of the level she had come from. Catalina entered and rode the elevator from the middle of the ship to the top.

The bulk of the *Artemis* was massive. Most of the Earths had sports arenas that were smaller than the *Artemis.* It was shaped like an oval cut in half-longways. The flat, rear of the ship housed its bacterial engines, composters, and Bubbledrive engine, leaving the majority of the huge area for the living library. As Catalina rode the elevator up the rounded front of the *Artemis,* she marveled at the different levels of the ship. The bottom layer of the ship comprised its laboratories, then came five levels of terrariums of every size, some designed to house a single specimen of insects, others devoted to breeding them by the tens of thousands. Going up from there, the gravity switched ninety degrees, so to an outside observer someone in the elevator would switch from being "upside-down" to "sideways" if they stopped in the middle of the ship because the gravgens of the aquatic level pulled all the water towards the engineering section at the back of the ship. After five levels of this (though these levels were flipped, see) the elevator would rotate another ninety degrees and finally the rider would appear "right-side up" as they rose past the five floors devoted to plant life in all its fecundity, and then the top floor which housed the ship's rather small bridge as well as the gym, cafeteria, media rooms, and official living and guest quarters. Catalina, having entered the ship halfway up, bypassed all this switching and spinning around, for the gravity on the cargo vessels was oriented the same way as the bridge was. Catalina loved to ponder this puzzle of gravity. It was bizarre to ground worms, perfectly logical to the engineers who'd had to design the ship's plumbing to work with artificial gravity, and almost completely unnoticed to someone aboard the *Artemis,* for each change in orientation of gravity happened inside of an airlock shaped like a sphere that simply rotated its passenger to the correct orientation. The elevator pinged and opened its door to the top level. Catalina exited and was on the bridge.

She found Fin sitting in her pilot's chair, swiveled backwards and staring at Catalina as she entered the bridge.

'Fin, what are you doing?'

33

'Captain Mondragon, I've been expecting you, sir.'

'Oh?'

'Sir. I believe I know why you are here.'

'Enlighten me, pilot.'

'We've been under Bubbledrive almost a week. I wish I could say I flew in a straight line but with gravity wells to dodge from the stars it was definitely not. At this point, it could be argued that we're either heading to Juxor or Earth-1, but from here on out it's going to be pretty damn obvious what we're going to do. So that's why you're here, you've got to decide. What'll it be, Captain? The polluted wasteland of Earth-1 to ditch your ex-boyfriend the entomologist or onwards to Juxor post-haste to get eaten by crabs?'

'Don't speak of Ensign Jupiter in that way again. Some infractions from Farah or Ikamon are to be expected; after all they knew me when we were together, but you were still in flight school and cheating on your ecological exams when Roman and I dated.'

Fin blushed so fiercely her skin was momentarily brighter than her dyed hair. 'Yes, sir. Sorry, sir.'

Catalina smiled inwardly, though her face remained an impassive scowl. Her ship was crewed with three of the most gifted ecologists the Institute had ever seen; she didn't much care that a pilot as skilled as Fin couldn't tell a moth from a butterfly, but Fin need not know that.

'But you are correct. When you present the problem that way it doesn't sound like much of a choice at all.'

'Yessir. Well, I would like to say it was nice knowing him. Hopefully the Institute will have a replacement, I guess. I'll drop from Bubbledrive near Tanagra and send your message into the comm relays. They should be able to send it by Bubblephone to Earth-1, so the general will know to expect us.'

'We won't be going to Earth-1, pilot.'

'Captain?'

'As I said, you made my choices very clear. Save a world from a problem we are uniquely qualified to solve, and may need Jupiter's expertise on, or abandon those colonists and deny our crew the man we may need most when we return to Epsilon-V.'

'Sir, yes, sir. Redirecting course for Juxor.'

'Aren't you forgetting something, Fin?'

'Sir, if we're not going to be strictly following orders I can make the necessary adjustments to our course under Bubble. No reason to drop into Tanagra's radio space and let the bosses back on Earth-1 know we're going rogue until we have to, right?'

'You couldn't be more wrong, pilot. I have a full report detailing Roman's heroic efforts on Wholhom and my reasons for keeping him aboard this vessel, as well as the duties he can perform as punishment for desertion. What planet are you from, pilot?'

'Mecha-Earth, err, Earth-3, sir.'

'Then you owe your very existence to the Institute. Never forget we are sworn to uphold the Charter. The Institute is the only thing out here giving the colonists a chance at air, water, and soil or sea. You will not speak of abandoning them or mention going rogue for as long as you are on an Institute vessel, is that clear?'

Fin stammered a sir yes sir and dropped the ship from Bubbledrive. Catalina filed her report and then the flashing lights of Interstellar travel returned. Catalina hoped Fin believed her bluster about her faith in the Institute, because she was doubting it more and more each day.

5

Three days later, Catalina stepped from the landing vessel of the Artemis and onto a metal dock suspended meters above the waves crashing below. They could have taken the skylift down to the surface and saved on fuel costs. Not many planets had one of the tethers that reached from the surface up past geosynchronous orbit and allowed cargo, people, and even ships to be transported by elevator to the surface and back. But Catalina felt she couldn't risk the few days that it would take. It had already been nearly two weeks since they'd received Juxor's distress call. Catalina could only guess what halting operations had been doing to the planet's economy.

At the far end of the dock, silhouetted by light glowing from a low squat structure, was a solitary figure standing on a platform in front of a group of men wearing long coats and high boots. Catalina saluted the man in front, but he didn't respond. He seemed to be yelling at the men and couldn't be bothered to greet the people who'd come from another planet to see him.

'You think that's them?' Farah Relkor yelled over a crack of thunder.

'It stands to reason,' Ikamon said. Catalina could almost feel Farah roll her eyes.

'Come on. Leave the gear for now.'

Roman didn't need to be told twice; he dropped the crate of shore grass seeds Farah had made him cart around and stood behind Captain Mondragon. 'Right, let's go meet the welcome committee.'

Captain Mondragon marched down the deck, her black boots clacking sharply even in the rain. Her crew followed, trying to keep their shoulders back and as straight as their captain's. By the time they had covered the fifty meters from the landing pad to the structure, they were all soaked to the bone. Catalina didn't let those assembled notice her discomfort. She still looked amazing in her wet uniform as she saluted crisply. The man speaking was older, his brow wrinkled to accommodate his scowl. It was hard to see him in the rain. He ignored her and continued his speech.

'I know those monsters are out there, and I know that's not what a lot of you signed up for, but think of what your bravery and sacrifice means for those that continue to serve the Carbon Man! Think of how the Mothers of the Ocean will thank you when you return, men who risked their lives for these living beauties fashioned from carbon and water. Who knows? The Mothers of the Ocean might just take you all!' The man unfurrowed his brow and lowered his voice, forcing the men to lean in if they wanted to hear over the roar of the wind. 'And believe me, you want the Mothers to take you. Think of all the work you've done for the Carbon Man out there, shoveling sludge, fixing machines, helping this planet not just survive but *contribute* to the Seeded Worlds. There's a place, my friends, that only the chosen may go, where the Mothers work just as hard, though their gift to Carbon is a different one. While you toil in the sludge, they watch and judge to see who among you can join them and help in spreading carbon as deep into the cosmos as we can!' The man gestured across the choppy bay to a huge, white building nestled high above the crashing waves. Even from this distance, one could tell it was a beautiful place, filled with tall trees instead of the scraggly weeds and grasses that clung to the rocky island they were on. It had gorgeous plazzglass windows that radiated light onto the heavy clouds about it.

'It's all bullshit!' one of the men called out and a few others grumbled.

'I promise you it's not. They are nymphs of the sea, embodiments of Mother Ocean herself that punish the wicked and reward the just. Has anyone here tasted the ambrosia of their sweet palace?'

A few of the men raised their hands.

'Tell our detractors here if it's real.'

'Oh, it's real, and goddess is the word for them. It's a place unlike anything you've seen outside the Earths. A palace! And it's just filled with food, beer, and gorgeous women, women like you would not believe, and all they want from you-'

'Is to work hard for the Carbon Man and Mothers of the Ocean? At least that's what they told me men who wished to return thought,' the leader said.

The worker nodded. 'That's right. You gotta work here, serve the Carbon man, and maybe get a taste of the Mother.'

The men grinned at each other.

'You risk your life just as our last crew did, but worry not. We have thousands of men working, and have only lost a few dozen. If something tragic befalls you, your next of kin will be sent recompense for the credits we owe you. With these crabs, we're willing to double that, but I might add that every one of your contracts had these clauses even before these demons appeared. You all knew this job had grave dangers and vast rewards. You are doing your part to *be* the Carbon Man, and if the Mothers of the Ocean don't thank you, he will. Go now, mourn those we've lost, but know that for every life spent on this planet, a dozen bloom forth on another, and that your hard work does not go unnoticed.'

The men headed off for a transport. Only two stayed behind, the older man addressing the crowd, and a younger man wearing a lab coat that was as thoroughly drenched as Catalina's own uniform. The rest of the men loaded on the ship and took off. It seemed either the detractor had been convinced.

Only then did the man turn his bald head towards the crew of the *Artemis.*

'Captain Catalina Solaris Xao Mondragon and crew reporting to a distress call from Juxor. This is my botanist and first officer Farah Relkor, Officer Ikamon our marine biologist, and Ensign Roman Jupiter our entomologist. We all must grow for the Charter,' she saluted crisply, not letting this man see her discomfort.

He watched her. He had hard silver eyes and stubbly cheeks. While the workers who'd loaded onto craft had been wearing black coats his was dark brown, nearly red, and thick. It looked very fine. He said nothing to them. After a moment the man in the lab coat cleared his throat and answered, 'The Charter grows because of us.' He was a bookish type and looked distinctly uncomfortable in the rain. His black hair was soaked and matted into his eyes.

'Took you long enough to get here,' the older man said and scowled, then turned his back to them and marched inside and out of the rain.

Catalina raised an eyebrow to her crew and gestured for them to follow.

Once inside, they found themselves in a wide room lined with rain slickers and boots. The old man was removing his rain cloak. It really was different than the rest. Most seemed to be made of a thick, black plastic, probably a carbon composite, but his appeared to be rich leather. It was emblazoned with a symbol. Twelve were spheres clustered tightly together and surrounded by two rings. The inner ring had two smaller spheres along it and the outer ring had four.

'It's the diagram of a carbon atom,' Ikamon murmured.

Catalina realized that indeed it was.

'Isn't that supposed to be some kind of religious symbol?' Roman asked.

Farah nodded. 'Yeah. Nutjobs think the whole universe was built for carbon to conquer. Think we're but messengers of the molecule.'

The dark-haired doctor approached the crew. 'You'll have to forgive him. He just conducted a funeral for the men lost in the latest raid.'

'I'm sorry to hear that,' Catalina said, then louder, so the older man could hear, 'you have my condolences. We have also lost someone to evolution run rampant. We are here to help on behalf of the Institute.'

The old man turned on them. His eyes were set deep in his skull behind a battalion of creases and wrinkles. He had a hard chin and a harder stare. 'And where were you a week ago when we lost eight more good men?'

'Under Bubbledrive, travelling here as quickly as possible,' Catalina said cautiously.

'Well it wasn't quick enough was it? Too bad the Institute couldn't send a faster ship.'

Catalina clenched her jaw, but said nothing. There was little to do for a man grieving. Already, she had misgivings about this man, not least of which was that he was wearing his religious cloak over his uniform for the Institute, but she knew now was not a time to question neither his loyalty to the Charter nor his religious beliefs. Farah, though, had none of the captain's tact.

'We are here to speak with one Targus Kane. He is listed as acting marine biologist, and must be your superior. Please take us to him and use this time to change out of your uniform. You shouldn't be conducting a religious service at all; to do it in your own uniform demands disciplinary action from your superiors,' Captain Mondragon said, eyeing the man's cloak. It was against the Charter for Interstellar Ecologists to preach religion, especially the new ones based on the existence of the 51 Seeded Worlds. The founders of the Institute decided that it simply wouldn't do for their scientists to be in the business of converting the people whose lives they had saved. Clearly, Targus Kane didn't read that part of the Charter often, if he let his officers conduct services in their uniform.

'My apologies,' the doctor stammered, 'This is Targus Kane, acting marine biologist of Juxor and head of the Church of the Carbon Man.'

'Mmm... I thought I recognized him,' Ikamon mumbled.

'Do you mean to tell us that you still have men out there working even after you sent that shitshow of a distress call through the comms? What, did you think those monsters were just going to forget how to kill?' Farah said.

'This is not some outer planet devoid of ladybugs or seagrass, *botanist*,' Kane hissed, 'I am the marine biologist of *Juxor*, which possesses the richest deposits of carbon ever discovered on a terrestrial planet. Without our production, the inner worlds would have shortages of plastics, lubricants, synthetic fuels, and carbon filaments. Three worlds owe their skylifts to the vast resources we control. I was tasked with keeping the seas of this planet fishable, yet we have discovered than an ocean of resources far richer than flesh lies beneath our troubled

41

waters. If I do not risk the lives of my men the outer worlds will grind to a halt.'

'I apologize for the impertinence of my crew, but do not think that out time in Bubbledrive was not spent studying with Juxor. The only piece of data still missing from the records is why a man of your obvious import is still listed in interstellar records as Juxor's *acting* marine biologist.'

'Our seas are almost the same composition as Earth-1's once were. They are rich in fish, oysters, shrimp, and squid. No one on this planet starves. The Institute has not sent some fish-monger to replace me because they appreciate the work I am doing to utilize the carbon reserves of this planet and strengthen mankind's hold on the cosmos,' Kane said.

'Except you are unfamiliar with the marine organisms that are harming your resources and killing your men?' Roman Jupiter said.

Kane scowled deeply, 'The crabs elude my expertise, though the men I spoke to at the Institute assured me that nothing like these monsters have ever been observed on the Seeded Worlds.'

'And how is that assuring?' Farah said.

It took much of Catalina's professional repose to keep her grin hidden.

'It means your *Institute* is doing its job if this is the first one of these mess-ups yet to happen.'

'I would have you remember that *our* Institute and the Charter we stand for are all that is keeping the Corps at bay. Without the protection of the Charter, your world would be up for grabs to whatever planetary government or corporation could land more colonists than you have and prove they provided them with air, water, and soil or sea, Catalina said. 'If that were to happen, the carbon reserves wouldn't belong to you anymore.'

'You disgrace me, Captain Mondragon. I'd have thought someone of your pedigree would know her history better. Even in your father's time, this planet was wealthy beyond what the other planets could hope to bed. Industry here is unparalleled amongst the inner worlds. Only Earth-3 compares to our ability to manufacture. Our faith has grown this planet into something powerful. Our influence spreads far and wide. No planet nor Corp would risk our wrath, for to anger us is to cut off one's supply of carbon! No one would dare lose access to such an essential element.'

'Except a bunch of locusts, you mean,' Roman said.

'Locusts?' Kane turned to the entomologist.

'Your whole operation is on the risk of crumbling to pieces because of an arthropod you don't understand. Much like the ancient emperors of Egypt and Rome, your power rests upon but one resource, in their case grain, in yours carbon, and now the proverbial locusts are here, the alleged crabs, and you can't do a thing about it. I apologize if I was unclear about the historical metaphor I was referring to.'

'Jupiter, stop talking,' Catalina said, but before she could attempt to rough over the damage her crew had already done, another voice proceeded to make it far worse.

'Did you notice what he said, Kane? *Alleged* crabs! Scientists from the Institute have been here a mere ten minutes and already they put forth hypotheses you have obsessively denied. The DNA sequence of those organisms isn't anything like a crab I've ever seen! And no crab has claws that can cut metal.' The woman faced the crew of the *Artemis*.

'Targus Kane has neither credentials nor accreditation from any intellectual organization, The Institute or otherwise. He is a greedy, petty individual who intends to use the carbon of Juxor, the perspiration of hard working men, and the apathy of our women to grow exceedingly rich. He is a sexist, a laughable excuse for a biologist, and a false prophet who doesn't even believe his own silly religion. You won't get anywhere talking to him.' The woman stopped speaking to catch her breath. She was around 170 centimeters, with frizzy, red, hair hardly weighted down by the rain, emerald green eyes, and a smattering of freckles across her nose. As soon as she stopped speaking, her smile cracked and it became quite clear she was embarrassed, yet she held her ground.

'And who are you?' Farah asked.

'I'm the most educated person on this sinking planet and the only person who has any idea about what those creatures really are. Osha McKenna, I hold doctorates in medicine, organic chemistry, and poetry, pleased to meet you.' She presented some sort of curtsy to top off the aberrant show of behavior.

Only Roman had the nerve to say anything, 'Charmed.'

Captain Mondragon seized the unusual moment of silence. 'Officer Relkor, Ikamon, see if there's any credence to this woman's claims. Jupiter, you're with me. Mr. Kane, I would like to see the last place this happened and any specimens of the organisms if you have them.'

The complaints were instant.

'Don't you think it would be better if I go with the strikingly gorgeous doctor?'

'Are you really going to leave me with her and Ken? Marine talk is boring.'

'I assure you there is nothing credible about anything Osha says.'

'I think perhaps I should see the specimens as well, you know?'

'Where should I go?'

Captain Mondragon only answered Dr. Fisk's question. 'You're with Kane and me, Dr. Fisk. As for the rest of you, those are my orders, understood?'

All three crew members saluted crisply, 'Understood, Captain.'

Only Kane brokered further argument. 'I assure you that Osha's theories are circumstantial at best. She doesn't know her place on this planet and is always trying to find ways to undermine my authority, and the authority of the planetary council.'

'Seeing as how she has clearance to your landing facility and you haven't told me that her credentials are fakes, she seems an important resource to this planet and my crew if we are to solve your problem.'

Kane grumbled, but he at least it was quiet.

'Perfecto.'

6

This was how Catalina found herself speaking with a nearly unspeakable man.

'So you see, we can't simply stop drilling. The demand for our resources is too high. The quicker you solve whatever your people messed up here, the better,' Kane said, his craggy face twisted into a cruel smile.

'Mr. Kane, the Institute hasn't done anything to this planet without the permission of your planetary council since it was established here 60 years ago,' Catalina said.

Kane scowled. 'And yet you come here lording your precious little badges over me. Don't think I don't know who you are or who your father was. This place predates the Charter, don't you try to take it away from us in the name of your Institute.'

'You sent out a distress call, we were the closest ship with a captain who thought her crew and vessel capable of addressing these creatures. Whatever is happening is undoubtedly some fluke of evolution unique to the conditions on this world. Believe me when I say my crew are the very best and that we will not rest until we solve this problem.'

'And what happens if you do? We'll have to pay up, correct?'

'It is customary to pay the Institute for our services. Without some source of income the organization would not be able to send crews on these rescue missions. The Institute may have been founded by millionaires and dreamers, but I assure you those of us still working for it a century later are far more pragmatic.'

Kane scoffed. 'And if we don't pay?'

'There are grants available for the less-prosperous planets. I would be happy to help you apply for a need-based charity.'

'Don't patronize me, Mondragon. Every man on this planet makes good money and the women live like queens. You know, you don't look too weak either, Ensign,' Kane said, turning to Jupiter. 'You want to earn some credits while you're here? We're always in need of men with strong backs. We'll pay you for your time, of course. Wouldn't want to risk any litigation and have your people send in more damn Interstellar Ecologists to ruin our way of life here. Just feels a little funny, paying you people to take care of a problem you caused.'

'Our records indicate Juxor never paid the Institute for the life in your seas, despite being originally populated by a Seedpod and later by ecologists who stocked your oceans with various tuna, sardines, anchovies, and shrimp. Rumor has it the oceans of Juxor are so rich a man in a rowboat can dredge enough food to feed a family,' Catalina said.

'Our oceans are quite abundant,' Kane grumbled.

'The men that don't work capturing carbon are easily able to feed the rest of our population,' Dr. Fisk said.

'Captain, a question,' Jupiter said.

Catalina nodded.

'I have noticed that you continue to refer to the working population of your planet as *men,* even though this particular euphemism has been replaced by *people* on most worlds. Tell me, is your world some sort of reverse ant colony, where the men toil and the women relax? Or is it more like a population of silkworms, genders toiling side by side, their hard work indistinguishable to such a degree that you prefer to call them all men, much as how I address my captain as sir despite her feminine characteristics?'

Catalina sighed. Feminine characteristics. It was hard to imagine that a few days ago when they'd been under Bubbledrive, Roman had been fawning over her feminine characteristics. One look at that Osha McKenna and he'd forgotten all about his love between the stars. Typical. She hoped he'd have more to contribute than arguing semantics with Kane.

'Oh, well, women on Juxor don't need to work,' Dr. Fisk mumbled.

'Roberth, don't demean what they do for our world and our church. Women have a far more important job than fishing or capturing carbon. The church of the Carbon Man teaches it as gospel, but I forget so many offworlders don't pay homage to whom we all owe our existence. Women on our world do not work because they have a more important task. Our planet is a utopia for our women. So long as a woman is using the greatest ability granted to her by the carbon element, she need never work.'

Catalina clenched her jaw tightly. Now she understood Dr. McKenna's fury at this man. She couldn't believe this. She'd heard men talk this way about women before. Cloning human beings had never caught on. It was unethical because it would give those wealthy enough to afford it an advantage that could last generations, not to mention the whole clones' rights debate. Besides that, though, cloning simply wasn't as efficient or effective as the alternative. Something about a slew of uninhabited worlds set men's minds to thoughts of the womb that were decidedly pre-equality. Jupiter, though, perhaps unfamiliar with this constant pressure from the other gender, had to ask.

'And what task is that?'

'Why, birthing and raising children, of course,' Kane said, his wrinkled and gnarled face breaking into a smile for this first time.

7

Ikamon didn't know what he'd gotten himself into. Osha McKenna was an organic chemist, a good, old-fashioned human medical doctor, and apparently, a poet, but a marine biologist she was not. Her theories were grand and outlandish, and decidedly broader than Kensei's laser-focused schooling he'd endured to win Farah's heart. Already the conversation had moved from biology, to ecological evolution, and on to that most testy of subjects, human evolution. Farah and McKenna were sitting in the back and Kensei was in the front seat monitoring the AI pilot the craft. The girls' conversation was decidedly off topic. McKenna has assured him that she'd show him her own samples of the creature, but as they flew over the archipelagos that made up the planet, Ikamon was losing hope that the pair would ever return to talking about marine life.

'This is un-fucking-believable!' Farah said over the ship's comm systems. Kensei considered turning them off, but with nothing but storm clouds, ocean waves, and drab islands to break up the monotony, he didn't.

'It is quite refreshing to hear that. Even my own sister thinks it a fair and equitable system. And it is, I suppose, if that's what one wants to do, but I'm not ready to spend my life attempting to procreate,' McKenna said.

'I hear that. Evolution's great and all, but that's for colonists. I can't imagine being forced to have children. That's one of the reasons I joined the Institute,' Farah said.

'Men don't expect that of you in space?'

Farah laughed. 'The only man who might dare mention children to me is my husband, Ken, but he's not that kind of man. Not threatening, that one.' Farah laughed and McKenna joined her, though more nervously.

Kensei sighed and continued to pilot the *Arrow* towards the destination McKenna had plugged into the ship's computer.

'Ken's idea of commitment is brewing a beer and letting it ferment for six months, or releasing some smelly fish into an ocean and coming back years later to eat it. Sometimes I miss being chased, but I'm appreciative that I got a man like poor Ken to lighten up the trips between the stars. I can't imagine being expected to procreate, though, and with multiple partners? Ken can be tiring enough, and he's just one.'

'It's not as if I'd actually have to spend much time with the fathers of my hypothetical slew of children. My sister certainly does *not*. She just picks a different man every year, they uh... they, well...'

'Boink like rabbits?'

'Yes, certainly,' McKenna said, 'they uh, *boink* until she's pregnant, then she sends the individual back to the sludge mines and returns to her life in the Fortress. Please don't misunderstand me. I love my nieces and nephews. All of them are smart and strong, since women here only pick the best. I should be happy with it; if I raised children I would be entitled to free rent, free food, free education, a free life. There's a certain logic to it, and it's empowering in a way, to see women in charge of their reproductive choices, and there are advantages to valuing women like

51

this. The last man moronic enough to rape a woman was thrown into the Portal decades ago. Our planetary council is filled with women, so women are key in directing the growth of this planet and the worlds that rely on our carbon. But I find it absolutely frustrating that no one respects me simply because I don't...that is procreation isn't my...I just won't boink them! None of the other women on this planet have two doctorates, let alone three. Growing children at the exclusion of all other activities is a waste of their potential, and a waste of mine!' McKenna sounded more like the woman they'd first met when she didn't have to talk about sex, Kensei thought.

'You ever consider leaving this place?' Farah asked.

'I couldn't possibly. Not with these creatures killing people. I was born here, my sister's raising her family of sludge-miners here. Even if you get rid of these things, this is my home.'

'Maybe it's better to stay. I mean, men are dogs. Spacers too.'

'What about your husband?'

'What, Ken?' Farah laughed. 'If he's a dog at least I got him trained after all these years. No new tricks, that's for sure. But there's dogs in space for sure. I'd tell you to ditch your family of, what did you call them, sludge-farmers? But we got one on our ship, a real mongrel.'

'The man who came with you? I admit I noticed him leering at me.'

'If he has his way I'm sure he'll pollinate every flower on this planet.'

'What do you mean?'

'It's just the way he talks. He's a bug guy, always going on about insects like he thinks he's a damn poet.'

'Oh. I've never met a poet. He writes poems about insects? We only have a few species of insects here.

52

Dragonflies, a few moths, and fireflies on a few of the islands that actually have grass.'

'Did you say fireflies?' Kensei said.

'Damn it, Ken, was this thing on?'

'Another planet he is right about. They are everywhere, you know? Despite not being on the Seedpods or in any Institute records.'

'They're not much use to us here. Same as the dragonflies. Probably released by one of your people years ago. But we have arrived! Please land, Mr. Ikamon.'

Kensei obliged, trying not to feel like the beaten dog. If there were only a few kinds of insects here, the crabs couldn't be one of them, and if they weren't, then Kensei knew what they had to be. If he'd have known Farah didn't care about his interstellar feasts, this entire problem might have been avoided. It seemed there was much about his wife he didn't know.

8

'If you've ever considered having children, Juxor would be a great place to plant your seed. Someone with your build and probable intelligence might be able to sire a dozen children before he leaves.'

Catalina felt her heart flutter once more for Roman Jupiter when he glanced at her and raised an eyebrow. She had expected him to jump at the chance to procreate with a planet of women. His deferment to his captain, who he did not currently lust after, was a refreshing surprise. Catalina almost imperceptibly shook her head. This was not a fight she was going to get into. If the people here were happy, it was no business of hers if the men were labor slaves and the women moderately educated breeders. It was a better life than many colonists had, and a better life than many of the people too poor or stubborn to leave Earth-1.

'Ah, quite,' Roman began awkwardly. 'I'm not one to pollinate so many flowers in one patch of earth, so to speak, yet this arrangement does make me curious. I wonder, does that vibrant Osha McKenna we met look to procreate traditionally?'

Kane scoffed. 'I don't even know why we're speaking of that insufferable brat. Probably a lesbian anyway, abomination to the church despite her sister being a member of our council, and having mothered seven children from seven men. Pushing the limits of evolution, that one, and yet we are all forced to suffer Osha because of the very reason she doesn't belong in our society. The council says that someone with her level of education has a right to weigh in on strategies to help this planet, and yet it is only because she has rejected the policies of this planet and refused to have children that she has such an education.'

'Mr. Kane, we are here to solve your ecological crisis, not condone or condemn your way of life. Now, if you would please take us to the site we can get on with saving your *men* and ensuring that your women are doing more than making crab food,' Catalina said. She was entirely finished with this conversation.

Doctor Fisk piloted the ship in a large circle around one of the larger islands and landed somewhere near the middle. There wasn't much to see in the way of ecology. A species of something like Bermuda grass had taken hold, but there were no other plants Catalina could see. Definitely nothing with flowers. There appeared to be no insect life except for tiny moths and the dragonflies that hunted them between fat drops of falling rain. It seemed most of the life of Juxor stuck to the oceans.

A load slap punctuated the roar of the crashing waves and gentle murmur of the rain.

'You have biting moths.' Roman held up the palm of his hand to show the smashed wings of said moth.

Dr. Fisk nodded. 'Yes, they have been here from almost the beginning. They are evolved, we think, from a fruit-piercing moth, but as our planet has little in the way of fruit, they learned to bite when the colonists first arrived. We'd be overrun if not for the dragonflies that eat them.'

'Biological controls at their finest,' Roman said.

'We wouldn't have any need for a biological control if the Institute hadn't dumped the damn moths out here in the first place. Why would any world need a moth that destroys fruit anyway?'

Roman shrugged. 'Silk production is an advantage of a fruit-eating moth, perhaps those that loaded the Seedpods a century ago took inspiration from them. You must remember that other planets have seas so crowded with clams that ships are unable to spin their propellers, yet here on Juxor your people couldn't function without this vital source of protein. The Seedpods were filled with many things, and given the richness of this planet, biting moths seem but a small price to pay. But tell me, where do they lay their eggs?'

Dr. Fisk's eyes lit up. 'Fantastic question. The moths lay them inland, of course, in what decaying matter they can, but the dragonflies prefer freshwater streams on the islands. For years we thought they were spreading from island to island during their adult phase and reproducing whenever they found the flies, but Dr. McKenna proved this to be untrue. She was able to demonstrate that some of the nymphs have evolved gills that function in the salty water of our oceans. Records indicate all the dragonflies released were freshwater species, and yet these ones can live in the salty ocean! McKenna discovered the difference, so we call them fiery dragonflies, despite their drab appearance.'

'Charming,' Roman said. Catalina recognized the amorous tone of voice. So he didn't want to breed with the whole planet, just McKenna.

'What does any of this have to do with anything?' Kane demanded. 'I have men dying and an Interstellar supply chain to fill, and you two are debating dragonflies? We don't have time for this. We need to get back to the creatures that did this to my men, not some irrelevant insects.'

Catalina looked at Roman, wondering if he'd figured something out, but he only shrugged and nodded. 'You're right of course, sir. Neither of these species did this to your people,' Catalina said. 'Take us to where it happened.'

They crested a small rise in the island and found the site. Catalina recognized it from the holo they'd watched back on the *Artemis*, but nothing else about the scene was familiar.

The machinery was in pieces. Metal pipes were cut as if they were twigs. The big generator was riddled with holes and covered in black filaments that looked like some dark, otherworldly spider webs. There was nothing left of the men's bodies save their bones, and even those had scratch marks and in places were nothing but white powder. Here and there the crab-like creatures still scurried about. Their little claws worked furiously, then they chewed for a moment before spitting out the black silk. Where the hole in the earth had been was now a mess of the black webbing.

'You're sure those organisms won't return?' Captain Mondragon enquired.

'Positive,' said Kane. 'They've only ever killed during thunderstorms. The few stragglers are peaceable enough.'

'Dr. McKenna hypothesized that the creatures are consuming carbon and can somehow sense high concentrations of it. It is unlikely our presence here compares to the buffet of a fresh find of carbon slurry. We believe that exposing the slurry to the surface stimulates some sort of feasting mechanism, to which they respond en masse. We don't understand much of the process because they somehow always time their emergence with strong thunderstorms that ruin our equipment. This is what we find when we return, a few survivors tending to this webbing, which is some sort of carbon composite, very complex stuff, stronger than steel, but very flexible.'

'What a fascinating hypothesis the Doctor had,' Roman said, unfolding a plazzglass cube and carefully guiding a crab into it, dodging its pincers. The creature went about its business, laying the black silk from end to end inside the small chamber, seemingly oblivious to its loss of freedom. 'And you're sure they're eating each other?' Roman asked.

'Do you see any bodies?' Kane sneered.

Roman looked around and eventually conceded that no, he did not. 'Normally when creatures feast it's to prepare to mate. Are there eggs present here?'

'No, and Osha's fool hypothesis can't explain that, either.'

'And yet the doctor's hypothesis is good enough for us to come take fresh samples of the creatures that I watched kill a dozen men?' Catalina said, growing annoyed with Kane. McKenna was obviously invested in solving this problem, why did he insist on using her first name, as if she was a child?

'I did not say that all of Osha's ideas were worthless, just her central one,' Kane said.

'And what hypothesis is that?' Catalina inquired.

'I would prefer the two of your go about your business and figure out what has happened here before I taint your ideas with the malarkey running through Osha's mind. She is a bright enough scientist, when she sticks to her field, but study in one area does not mean it transfers to all others.'

'Mr. Kane, do not think that by telling our crew a theory it will occlude all others. We are a team of scientists who follow the facts we see before us. Roman Jupiter is a gifted entomologist, who I am quite certain will lend insights that are invaluable to this investigation. Ikamon and Relkor are even more skilled. Now, if Dr. McKenna's theories are valued enough for us to risk our lives by being in the presence of these creatures, I think it best we hear them in their entirety.'

'It would be best if we discuss it after you propose what you are thinking. Surely your Mr. Jupiter has a working hypothesis?' Kane said.

Catalina was eager to solve this problem if only to get away from this man. She did not like the way he spoke of McKenna and Jupiter, as if their genders demanded different levels of respect. Still, this was an important planet, Kane had the right of that. Their carbon exports made life easier on so many worlds, and if the women here were happy—and Catalina would be sure to follow up with the planetary council before she left—then she had no right to judge. Her work was in fulfilling the Charter, not upholding gender roles she believed in, much as it frustrated her.

Roman looked at the captain. Maybe he had an idea after all, but Catalina would not have him revealing it in front of this gender-biased zealot. She shook her head 'no,' so slightly as to be imperceptible.

'It's curious that the supposed crabs eat meat and spin webs, but no, no theory yet,' Roman said.

But then a touch of her faith in the opposite gender was restored, as bumbling Dr. Fisk spoke up. 'Surely we can tell them, I mean come on, it's ridiculous. They'd never guess it in a thousand standards unless we tell them.'

'Tell us what?' Roman said, growing eager.

Kane rubbed his face, but said nothing, so Dr. Fisk continued with a grin, 'Osha McKenna thinks that the crabs are aliens sent here to destroy us.'

9

'There is no other reasonable hypothesis. What else could they be?' Osha McKenna said.

Kensei scratched his head, unsure of where to even begin.

'You mean... besides aliens?' Farah started hesitantly.

McKenna nodded, her grin wide underneath the smattering of freckles on her nose.

Farah could not hold back, 'There are a thousand possible explanations. I know it may be hard to believe, but we've seen all sorts of new species on different worlds. Every Seedpod may have had the same mix of plants and animals, but in the hundred years since they've landed, life has evolved in strange ways. It's far more likely we're dealing with a new form of something from Earth-1 than an alien life form that's never been reported on any world surveyed by the Institute and was somehow introduced or lying in wait to attack the colonists of an inner world who have been here for decades.'

'Obviously the Institute is keeping this information classified,' Osha said, rolling her eyes. 'They don't believe the populace of the inhabited worlds can handle such a challenge to our assumptions. They think there would be riots if people knew the universe wasn't empty before *homo sapiens* emerged as the eminent interstellar species.

It would change the entire paradigm for organic expansion!'

'I don't think people would come to the defense of some flesh-eating crab, whether it's alien or not,' Farah said.

'*Eto…* it is possible that these crabs are from outside the typical evolutionary ladder, but I don't think your hypothesis is correct.' Kensei shook his head. 'It is possible someone with kind intentions released these things on your world and they mutated into these monsters.'

Farah looked sharply at Kensei, but he kept his gaze locked on McKenna. He wasn't sure that was what had happened, of course, but if it was it would be his duty to stop it. Though these flesh-eating crabs weren't any of the mollusks or fish from the Seedpods, nor were they any of the organisms ecologists had officially released in the years following the Great Seeding; they were still marine creatures, and thus his responsibility. Kensei wished he would have studied more about them than how to make a butter sauce for their claws.

'I have looked at that possibility and admit that it could be possible. I am aware such mutations happen. The forests of Guadalupe, for example, have unique birds and fruiting plants that evolved from the specimens Interstellar Ecologists released, but this is totally different. Look here,' McKenna said, gesturing towards a microscope.

Kensei put his eyes to the lens—anything to avoid the icy stare Farah was giving him. What he saw under the glass appeared to be a multi-faceted diamond.

'It appears to be a multi-faceted diamond,' Kensei said, scratching his head.

'It is a diamond!'

'What relevance does this have on the creatures?'

'It *is* the creatures! Or their claws, anyway. That's why our metals cause little hesitation for them. They have diamond-tipped claws. Now tell me you've seen that on another planet.'

Kensei shrugged, 'No, I have not seen that, but it is just carbon arranged in a new way. It is certainly possible; we have found diamonds on many worlds.'

'I knew people from the Institute would not be able to contemplate the validity of a hypoethsis so contradictory to their indoctrination. Please be honest with me. Is this hypothesis beyond your ability to reason, or do they pay you to keep quiet about it?'

Kensei raised his eyebrows.

'Surely you've seen things. When I heard an O-class was coming I read up on you. What happened on Epsilon-V? Where's the follow up on that, and what happened to Dr. Mercurian? There was no mention of anything bad happening to him, and yet here you are, halfway across the inhabited sector with some grinning moron masquerading as a green entomologist?'

'Jupiter is certainly a moron, but he *is* a good entomologist,' Farah said in resignation.

'Then what is happening here? What are you two trying to hide? I know that whatever is in the oceans cannot be explained by any hypotheses you've posited thus far. These crabs can smell carbon slurry from kilometers away, spin webs, and have diamond-tipped claws. It is simply preposterous to think that some foodie released a bunch of snow-crabs here and they went wild!'

'Is that what you think, Ken?' Farah said, her words pointed.

Kensei found himself backed against a wall, with two women far too smart for him battering his sensibilities. Fortunately, just then he remembered that he *had* seen something like before.

'The remnants of the aphids on Wholhom had carbon nanostructures for their proboscis that were as strong as diamonds, you know? Perhaps this is somehow related.'

'Ha!' McKenna was not deterred. 'A world away? Sounds like aliens to me, or espionage from the only thing that's been to both places. *You,*'

'Don't burn your bridges, sweetheart. I can assure you that *most* of the Institute had nothing to do with this, but don't ever doubt the rash actions of a desperate individual. We need to show this all to the captain. Come on, Ikamon.'

Kensei's shoulders slumped. Farah hadn't used his nickname since they'd first slept together so many years ago. Said it was unsexy, that she didn't want to bed a squid-man. Kensei supposed there was nothing sexy in his future, though, not if Farah had figured out what he had done.

10

'What do we know thus far?' Catalina asked her crew. They were in a room of the spaceport with a comm open to Fin back up on the *Artemis*.

'Well I would think it's fairly obvious by now. Ikamon would you like to do the honors?' Jupiter said.

'Yes. Ikamon. what exactly is happening on this ass-backwards planet, I mean besides institutionalized sexism?' Farah said.

'Might I remind you that our duty is to the Charter and to this world's ability to support life, not influencing the politics or gender norms of their society. Juxor hasn't had a problem in years save these crabs.'

'Alleged crabs,' Roman interrupted.

Catalina clenched her jaw and slowly took a deep breath. 'If not for these *alleged* crabs, we wouldn't even be here. We need to solve this problem, protect these people's right to air, water, and soil or sea, and make our way to Epsilon-V.'

'So you're not turning me in to Earth-1?' Jupiter asked.

'Oh we are definitely going to turn you in. It's the quickest way to Epsilon-V anyway,' Farah said.

'Actually, Captain, there is news on that front,' Fin said over the comm from the *Artemis* up in its orbit.

'Proceed,' Catalina said, wondering if a conversation with her crew could ever be straight-forward.

'The Institute upgraded the distress call of Juxor from orange to red, calling it a "real and urgent threat to all the Charter is sworn to uphold for Juxor and all the planets that Juxor supports." They've greenlighted our request to come here and send their confidence in you and hope that you can solve this matter as quickly as a crew of our reputation is expected to.'

'Well that's more like it!' Jupiter said.

'She's talking about us, not you, you ignoramus. You don't have a single badge besides your ensign pin.'

'I'll have you know that the captain put in a good word for me.'

Farah's red-hot eyes turned to meet Catalina's icy stare. For a moment nothing was said as the tension in the air crackled. Catalina prepared to send her botanist up the Space Elevator, but fortunately, Fin broke the silence.

'Actually there's news on that too. First Officer Relkor has been awarded a badge for her work on the fungus, and Captain Mondragon has been given a badge for saving the peanut crop and Wholhom's economy.'

There was a pregnant silence in the air for moment before Fin said, 'That's it. Sorry, Jupiter.'

'It's all politics,' Jupiter muttered. 'Stupid planet anyway. Bunch of moths would mistake a fire for the light of the moon.'

'You were in love with one of those moths a month ago!' Farah fumed.

'Who, Shay? I don't know. She seems fairly pedestrian compared to Dr. McKenna, don't you think?'

'Which brings us back to the matter at hand,' Catalina said, attempting to reorient her distractible crew. 'I assume we're all on the same page about McKenna's theory?'

'Ridiculously absurd.'

'Charmingly naïve, but ultimately incorrect, despite the Doctor's obvious brilliance.'

'There is a more obvious solution.'

Catalina turned to Ikamon. 'And that is?'

Ikamon took a deep breath and turned from his captain to his wife. 'I never thought I was worthy of you, you know? You are so passionate, so beautiful, and I was just a plumber-turned-Marine Biologist when we met. The only reason I was able to win you over was that meal on your parents' planet.'

'Earth-4 is *not* my parents' planet,' Farah said.

'The Relkors only own *half* of Earth-4,' Roman quipped.

'Either way. That has driven me all these years, you know? I live to delight your senses. The oysters on Graken, the calamari from Despar, the stinky sardines from Xochiquetzal I thought you enjoyed,' Ikamon took a deep breath, 'or softshell crabs.'

'Oh this is great. Just fucking great. So it's true, then? This is why you've been acting so weird, why you've been sulking, because this is all your fault!'

'Someone please enlighten me as to what Ikamon is talking about?' Catalina said.

'Just romance of the interstellar degree,' Jupiter said wistfully.

'If I'm getting this, and I'm quite sure I am because of the dumb, depressed dog look on my husband's face, Ikamon has been releasing specimens of marine life on every planet we go to in hopes of feeding me, because apparently that's all I care about.'

'Like the black widow, you have sucked all the love from your poor mate's heartfelt offer of food,' Roman said.

'Is this true?' Catalina said, turning to Ikamon.

66

'Yes, Captain.' Ikamon hung his head. 'My last visit here, a routine stop on the *Muir*, I released crabs into the ocean, hoping to woo Farah one day. It appears they have mutated over the years into these flesh-eating monsters. I have dishonored you and the Institute. I have brought shame to my family.'

'Oh don't be silly, Ikamon,' Jupiter said, 'we all do this kind of thing when we visit planets. On Wholhom I released those pipevine swallowtails, but I also introduced a queen ant and her brood of few hundred workers, and a couple dozen June bugs just to see what would happen. I mean, Comrade Relkor, surely you release wildflower seeds when you visit planets?'

'Don't answer that!' Catalina hissed. 'I would prefer that the majority of my crew is not in breach of the Charter and the rules of terraforming laid out by the Institute. How could you two be so stupid? This is exactly the reason why the release of new species is to be carefully logged and checked with HQ back on Earth-1. I expect this kind of thing from Jupiter, but from you, Ikamon? This is neglect bordering on insanity. And that I find out about it in a spaceport, where we can almost be certain that that unspeakable Mr. Kane is listening? You are both on probation starting this very minute and will not go anywhere on this world without supervison by someone qualified to keep an eye on this, this mutiny! Now, we will go about our business and solve this problem, is that understood?'

Jupiter and Ikamon both nodded. Farah, though, stood up fast enough as to knock her chair out from under her.

'No, that is not acceptable, Cat! I have told you time and time again about the dangers of taking this ingrate Jupiter on board with us. He was a mess on the *Carson* and he's worse now. If I had known that he was contaminating planets for fun and corrupting the man I *thought* I knew and loved, I would have made my opinions far more clear. I will not work with this *man*, nor will I work with that one,' Farah said, wiping a tear from her eye, 'in fact, Captain, until you can get your crew in order, I won't work for you, either. I quit!'

Farah fell into tears and stormed out of the room and off into the rain of Juxor.

'*Perfecto,*' Catalina said. 'Well, if there's nothing else, I guess we need to come up with a way to destroy Ikamon's crabs.'

'Yes, Captain,' Ikamon said, heaving himself to his feet.

'I'm sorry, Ikamon's crabs?' Jupiter said.

'Yes, Ensign. Or was that exchange not clear enough for you? Apparently your little experiments haven't had disastrous effects yet, but you'll be on probation all the same due to the risks being so apparent.'

'Captain, did I not make my hypothesis clear? I had only mentioned my releasing insects to help show that Ikamon's little foray into increasing biodiversity isn't to blame here. As you said, none of the creatures I released have mutated, not enough time in their new environments I would think. Ikamon's crabs could not have grown diamond claws in ten standards.'

'So then, you think it's aliens?' Ikamon stammered.

'No. Unfortunately for Dr. McKenna's and my soon-to-be working relationship, I find her hypothesis lacking. I thought it was quite obvious what is happening here, unusual, but obvious.'

'Enlighten us,' Catalina said.

'It's an insect, some sort of hybrid.'

'Impossible,' Ikamon said.

Jupiter shrugged. 'Unlikely, perhaps, and yet I find it far more likely than thinking it some snow crab that lost its legs, learned to spin web, and fly.'

Jupiter waited a moment, but when no one said a thing he raised an eyebrow. 'Captain, you didn't notice? I thought I had made it quite clear in front of Kane.'

'Well I wasn't there so make it obvious now,' Fin said over the comm.

'The two species of insects that are most abundant here, a moth and a dragonfly, have already developed quite remarkable adaptations. In what sounds like less than a year, the moth learned to eat flesh, a most unpleasant trait of the new organism to be sure, and the dragonflies evolved so that their nymph form could survive in the ocean, a unique though not unexpected development. What we are observing is a creature that has characteristics from both organisms. It survives in its nymph form in the seas, until it senses food. Then it surfaces to feed and spins a communal cocoon, similar though decidedly more advanced than silkworms. Once fed, they strip down and undergo metamorphosis into their adult form; they must fly off to their breeding ground, you see. Those that remain consume the carbon exoskeletons of their faster compatriots, clearly being creatures that are desperate for carbon. I admit the diamond claws are unusual, but given the complexity of carbon molecules on this planet it seems possible that these creatures, when undergoing their rapid changes, incorporated them much as animals do with their environments the worlds over. Like legendary elephants eating clay!' Roman said.

'But that's...that can't be,' Catalina said.

'Hmm...there are instances of different species hybridizing on Earth-1, but nothing so outlandish as a moth and a dragonfly,' Ikamon said.

'I admit, I haven't seen anything like it, either, but it really is the only explanation that makes sense. Perhaps a dragonfly captured a moth, and in state of excitement fertilized it and it dropped its eggs onto an island of just the right solar radiation to cause the proper mutations.'

'Ikamon, what do you think?' Catalina asked.

'I only have one question.'

Jupiter raised an eyebrow.

'Why did you not say all this before Farah ran off?' Kensei asked, his head sagging into his hands.

'Because I didn't want to ruin your gift to Farah. Spreading life in the name of love,' Jupiter smiled. 'How romantic! Pity she didn't see it that way, but not surprising.'

'I'll get Farah back. What I need to know right now is what plan do you have to get rid of these hybrids?' Catalina said.

'Thank you, Captain,' Kensei said, his normally light tone heavy with emotion. 'Yes, Roman, what is your plan?'

'Oh. I have no idea.'

Kane shut off the leak he'd installed in the room he'd given to the crew of the *Artemis*. It wouldn't do for them to discover he'd learned of their illegal activities through spying. People could be sensitive about that kind of thing. It was a pity the crabs weren't their fault. Hopefully they could still fix the problem, but in the process Kane would be sure to make sure to record whatever mistakes they made, or make some for them if they didn't. Either way the result would be the same. Juxor would take the *Artemis*, and Kane's influence would no longer be limited to the planetary council stuffed with a bunch of short-sighted and narrow-minded women.

11

Osha McKenna was impossibly annoyed. Obviously, something was wrong with the crew of the *Artemis.* She and Kane had been waiting outside their little private meeting. Kane was excited like a squid in a shrimp farm, surely spying or planning their demise or thinking about rolling around in a pool of sludge. She detested the man immensely, and yet had to work with him, for no one else on their planet seemed the least bit concerned that men were dying. It was almost as if they believed their carbon religion, that evolution was sculpting man with its most ancient of tools: death. Osha shuddered. She didn't like to think that humans were still susceptible to evolution as an outside force. She preferred to believe that knowledge and forethought were now sculpting the human genetic code, not dumb luck. She and her sister agreed on that point at least, though little enough else.

Osha was pulled from her thoughts as the botanist practically kicked open the doors from their room and marched off down the hallway, half sobbing and half mumbling angrily. Osha considered following her. She liked Farah. She was refreshing compared to the woman of Juxor—whose sole purpose seemed to be to grow more women—and yet she had to talk to the other two. A botanist wouldn't do much against the crabs.

A minute after that, the captain came out.

71

'Which way did my first officer go?' she demanded. Kane shrugged, so in reflex Osha pointed to the cable car door she'd loaded into.

'And that goes where?'

'To the home of the Mothers of the Ocean, the Carbon Man's noblest warriors,' Kane said.

'*Perfecto,*' Captain Mondragon said, clearly angry. She clenched her jaw and her sense of calm returned. 'She will be safe there?'

'Oh yes,' Kane beamed. 'And who knows? Maybe when you people think you have solved your problem, and wish to make for the stars, she'll chose to stay here, fulfilling The Carbon Man's destiny to spread our form of life throughout the universe.'

'Sure. Maybe,' Captain Mondragon said. Osha swore she could detect a smile underneath the captain's stony visage. 'Do you have a Bubblephone relay? I need to file a report and don't have time to go up to my ship.'

'Oh yes but of course, I can take you there. It's an older model, though, perhaps someone can help you transcribe your message?' Kane said.

'It's down the hall, third door on the left. The receiver's out past the planets, so sometimes it takes a while to get the message through. Tell the operator the red-headed fox sent you. He'll give you a minute alone with the machine. You'll do fine, I'm sure,' McKenna said.

'Must you try to block everything I do?' Kane demanded of Osha.

'If it thwarts the Institute, then yes!' McKenna said.

'Mondragon, I must insist that I accompany you, it would not do for you to be left alone. I wouldn't want you to come across a gang of our laborers and drive them into a frenzy.'

'She does look all right in that uniform, but surely if they can control themselves around the red-headed fox, a short, Colombian jaguarondi should present little problem,' Jupiter said. He was leaning on the doorframe to the room they had just been in.

Osha was aghast. Men didn't speak that way about women on Juxor, not unless they wanted to get thrown from the Portal. Captain Mondragon only clenched her jaw.

'Surely.'

Kane grinned widely. 'You would think so, but our men are familiar with seeing Osha in a slicker, filthy as the rest of them, while your captain looks so pristine. An unusual ray of sunshine on this rainy world.'

'But, sir, if you go with the captain, you won't have time to answer my own questions about your faith,' Jupiter winked at Osha as he said this.

'I assure you there is no reality to his claims. He believes that carbon will make him rich, that is all,' McKenna said.

'Sometimes there is an elegance even to the fruit fly. Mr. Kane, I've always been a believer in a tent of what you said earlier. I heard you tell your men that this planet is proof that the Carbon Man, a metaphorical god to be sure, exists because the very richness of it means we were meant to find it. Extrapolating this logic outward, do you also believe that the discovery of Bubbledrive and the asteroid mines on Earth-3 are proof that a benevolent spirit is out there?'

'Indeed. It is a central teaching of our belief,' Kane said as he nodded and turned to face Jupiter. In that moment, Captain Mondragon marched down the hallway and vanished into the room with the Bubblephone. Osha had no doubt that it would take her but a moment to send whatever message she needed to. Osha didn't know what to do. She wanted to pick the captain's brain about her work, but she also didn't want to interrupt her. This conversation between Jupiter and Kane was obviously going nowhere fast, but then, Osha had *never* heard anyone discuss the religion her sister and Kane believed in. It was always taught and preached, but never actually pondered, it seemed. And she liked that Jupiter had called him a fruit fly.

Kane continued, 'If the Carbon Man was malevolent, he would have left us on Earth-1, but instead we found what we were looking for, a way out of the solar system with Bubbledrive, and planets that could support our population a hundred times over. The abundance of the metals in the asteroid mines of Earth-3 is further proof that the Carbon Man gives us that for which we search. Without those metals we would never have built any Bubbledrives beyond those on the Seedpods and the few first ships that got us to the Earths. As soon as we wanted more of the metals to make Bubbledrive engines, as soon as our *faith* in the Carbon Man was strong enough, we were granted what we needed. Juxor is but the next iteration of that ability to fulfill our own destiny. The Carbon Man rewards faith in forward thinkers most of all.'

'But if the Carbon Man is so kind why is he killing people here, on this most blessed of his planets?' Osha countered, unable to bite her tongue.

'A brilliant point from the brilliant scientist,' Jupiter said.

'The Carbon Man does not preclude death from his methods. For without it, we could not grow. DNA is meant to break down, there's no doubt about this. We've hardly extended longevity past a century, and yet we've conquered solar systems. Death is one of his tools. We will work through it and be stronger because of it. You must remember how many people died to get us here, and yet here we are, exactly where we need to be, sitting on top of a planet rich in carbon and water.'

'This is where my question enters, I suppose, and perhaps what will make me a believer,' Jupiter said.

'It's all just motivation to get men to work. Converts must shovel sludge,' Osha said and rolled her eyes.

Kane, though, was practically watering at the mouth. 'Quiet, Osha! Let the man speak. I thought you said we owed those from the Institute some respect.'

'Like the respect you showed the captain?' but Osha then quieted down; she, too, was interested in what Roman was going to ask.

Roman looked back and forth between the two of them, almost as if the question was as much for Osha as it was for Kane. He winked at her again.

'I have found fireflies on every single planet I have ever visited. This is despite there being no fireflies on the original Seedpods, nor any records of them being released. And yet, they are on every world I have seen. No other insect, creature from the sea, or vascular plant can boast this claim to survival on every Seeded World. Indeed it seems that fireflies are spread even wider than mankind itself. They adapt to a variety of worlds, be it dry, moist, hot, or cold, and always have a thriving population hidden away somewhere. My question is this: if a god or the Carbon Man or whoever is responsible for all of the discoveries we make that we so dearly desire— be it oceans of usable carbon, Bubbledrive, or the Seeded Worlds—is it *He*, or a different higher power that is ensuring the survival of the fireflies?'

Kane said nothing. His mouth worked dumbly. He was entirely flabbergasted. Clearly, he had not expected his first serious conversation about his religion to be a joke!

Osha could control herself no longer. She let out a peal of laughter punctuated by a few snorts.

'Mother of the Ocean. I've been listening to this incorrigible idiot since I was a little girl, and never have I heard such a perfect refutation of his argument! He makes a good point, Kane,' McKenna said between giggles. 'Who's to say *why* your Carbon Man wants us out here? Maybe it's to catch fireflies!' Osha laughed so hard she snorted.

Roman smiled fondly at her as Kane fumed, trying to find words, but unable to do so.

After a delicious moment, Ikamon emerged from the room, drying his eyes it looked like, and approached Kane. 'I have some questions about your harvests, sir: what sort of things you've been catching, whether you've released any other species of crustaceans besides shrimp, your fish stocks, that sort of thing.'

'*You* dare to accuse *me* of releasing creatures on this world? I don't care what's in the damn oceans.' Kane said.

'Sir, you are the planet's acting marine biologist. If you cannot answer my questions I must request another marine biologist from the Institute.'

'No, it's fine,' Kane said, grinding is teeth. 'Last thing we need is to have to wait for another one of you.'

'Shall we, sir?'

'Yes, fine. This way Ikoma or whatever they call you.' Kane tromped off with Ikamon at his heels.

Osha found herself standing next to Jupiter. He smiled at her and nervously scratched his hair, messing it up.

'That was brilliant, what you did to Kane. Absolutely brilliant,' Osha smiled. 'Maybe you're not so bad.'

'I would greatly appreciate a chance to show you that I'm not. Perhaps we can use this time to go foraging? How many of your islands have you explored?'

'A fraction, honestly, most of them are too small to be of any consequence. What are you hoping to find? Oh I guess it doesn't matter, right? Whatever it is, we'll find it!' Osha cracked a smile and fell into laughter again.

'I find your laughter absolutely intoxicating,' Roman said.

'It is quite obvious that you do.' One did not hold a degree in poetry and fail to recognize flirtatious language. 'Come, let's take a transport, Romeo. It'll be better than being here.'

'Roman.'

'Hmm?'

'Not Romeo, my first name is Roman.' Roman smiled bashfully.

'It is a reference to a flirtatious character from one of Shakespeare's more enduring works. I use it here only because of your behavior towards me, and the obvious similarities in your names.'

'I know Shakespeare. I prefer to write sonnets to his iambic pentameter. Still, I prefer not to be called Romeo, if only to avoid the tragic outcome of that particular play. I prefer Roman, if you please.'

Osha rolled her eyes. The 'if you please' was a little much, but not enough to make her stay in the spaceport with the mopey marine biologist, and she'd do anything to put off visiting her sister in the Fortress. Osha found she could not wipe the smile from her face as she and Roman climbed into a transport vessel. Was this how Juliet had felt when first confronted with her beloved? Osha shook the idea from her mind. They had a planet to look after. Hopefully this Roman Jupiter's entomological skill would prove as formidable as his wit. Maybe then, when all this was over, she could ask to hear one of his sonnets.

12

Farah didn't know where she was walking, just that she didn't want to be anywhere near Ken or Roman or even Catalina right now. She switched off her comm, fighting back tears of betrayal by muttering under her breath about how she'd show them all. She came to a tube transport system, and without a second thought hopped in the transparent sphere and slapped a destination at random.

The sphere shot out from the spaceport and the tube enclosing it fell away. Farah was flying above the ocean, it seemed, protected by a transparent sphere that was tethered to a thin cable. Farah had heard about these, apparently a less efficient and less resource-intensive way of doing public transportation than an enclosed Hyperloop. The sphere she rode inside of was attached to a cable by magnetic locks that carried the plazzglass sphere with almost no friction. The effect was that the plazzglass ball Farah was trapped in shot out over the troubled waters of Juxor fast as almost any planetary transport she'd ever experienced. It certainly felt just as fast. She saw that, in the distance, the cable was anchored to another of the larger islands that made up the inhabited archipelago of Juxor. The Fortress, she thought she'd heard Kane say. Its tall, shining surfaces bespoke of the carbon filaments it was made of; its plazzglass windows a testament to mankind's first and most enduring triumph, its victory over the rain. The sphere Farah was traveling in reached its terminal velocity and a display near the cable up above blinked at her. Five minutes. It was an efficient ride, if nothing else.

Farah looked down below the sphere into the churning waters of Juxor. The seas were rich here: even from her height and speed she could see large shoals of fish being hunted by even larger species, perhaps one of the great tuna Kensei was always going on about. Oh Kensei, why hadn't he told her what he had done? To think he'd done it on the *Muir!* They'd been on that ship together. They'd been married on that ship! It made Farah sick to think that Kensei might have snuck off after one of his signature dinners to contaminate a planet's ecosystem on her behalf. She didn't remember coming to Juxor before, but she didn't have a memory for these things like Catalina did. Plus, the ecosystems of the Seeded Worlds could change so *fast.* That was why it was so important that everything the Interstellar Ecologists released was *documented.* If Ken would have just documented the release of the crabs in the ship's log and told his captain all those years ago, it'd all be so different!

But would it?

These crabs would still exist even if they were documented. Despite people having mastered the Bubbledrive and artificial gravity, available technology varied widely from world to world. Even on Juxor, a planet of industry and growing population, it was doubtful that anyone had bothered to manufacture submarines dexterous enough to hunt down thousands of crabs. Sure they had refineries and a public transport and places to stay dry, but all that technology had existed long before mankind had found the stars and given up on exploring the unknown depths of Earth-1. Farah sighed. No, even if Kensei had told his captain, this problem would still exist. The only difference would be Ken wouldn't be facing charges of planetary ecological destruction. Depending on the severity of the damage done by the crabs, Ken could face millions of credits in damages, which would surely get him ejected from the Institute, and that was assuming that the planetary council decided not to prosecute Ken for the murder of those men who'd died at the hands of his crabs.

'Damn you, Ken!' Farah shouted to no one. Didn't he know this could get him grounded? And for what? To impress her with a meal? Not that Farah didn't mind having her own personal chef serving up interstellar delights that probably no single human had tasted since the golden age of Earth-1. She sighed. Much as she liked the meals, she far preferred Ken's company. And then there was the sex. Farah didn't know what the hell she'd do without Kensei. It had been hard enough getting the man to rise to meet her kinky appetite; the idea of having to expose that part of herself to another man who would probably be far less understanding than Kensei was too much to bear. And yet, that was what she was going to have to consider. Ken had been lying to her for years, lying to the Institute. He could have put thousands of lives in danger, maybe millions! And for what? Certainly not for the Institute, this wasn't how they operated, but if not for them, then for... Farah sighed again. The moron had done it for love. Farah rolled her eyes. This was nonsense straight out of Roman Jupiter's book, not calm and clever Kensei's. It hadn't surprised Farah at all to discover that Roman disregarded protocol the first chance he got and released undocumented species on Wholhom. He'd probably encouraged Kensei to do it too. How she hated Roman Jupiter, the way he treated women like annuals—

something to be picked and enjoyed, then discarded for something prettier the next spring. What Farah and Kensei had was anything but annual. Their relationship was the deep roots of perennial love, and now it seemed Roman was jeopardizing even that. It wasn't enough for him to break the hearts of a dozen women on a dozen worlds, he had to break hers as well. Farah vowed that she would fix whatever was wrong with Roman Jupiter, and if that didn't work then she'd do everything in her power to pull him from her and her husband's life like a weed from an otherwise healthy garden.

The sphere Farah was riding in came to a gentle stop, no doubt magnet suspension as well, and Farah stepped from the sphere and looked around at where she was, making note of the return cable back to the spaceport. Not that it would be easy to get lost. Juxor's skylift reached all the way to geosynchronous orbit in space. It was well-lit and monolithic, a piece of mechanized perfection rising from the grungy spaceport.

Farah found herself in a building that was far nicer than the spaceport had been, with its muddy halls and endless rows of boots and rain slickers. Where in the spaceport, the labor of people was apparent, but the people missing—out working in the rain harvesting sludge no doubt—here the people were present, but showed no sign of labor. A pair of women walked past, wearing long, flowing gowns that exposed toned legs and arms. Their hair was done up elaborately with flowers Farah hadn't seen outside her parents' private gardens on Hot Earth. Three children trailed behind them, chatting animatedly. From the other direction came a man carrying a silver platter laden with drinks. His dark hair was long, combed to a shine and tied back neatly. He wore no shirt, and instead seemed to have traded it for body oil, for the muscles of his bronzed chest glistened. He approached

81

the women with a cordial smile, bowed politely, and offered them drinks from the tray. One of the women declined, but the other took a drink and bid the first woman to go on with the children.

Farah slowly walked closer, curious to hear what was going on.

'And tell me of your grandparents,' the woman said and smiled. Farah noticed she had a shock of curly red hair like McKenna.

'My mother's parents were both born on Earth-1. They worked hard to send my mom to a good school on Solar Earth. One of the Harvards. No health problems, no cancer or Alzheimer's or nothing like that. Good people. My mom tried to move them there with us, but it was expensive. She made it happen, but she's still in debt for it. That's why I'm here, really, help her pay that off.'

The woman smiled. 'Well that is admirable. It's a pity that moral fortitude isn't genetic so far as we can tell. And your father's parents?'

'My dad's dad died of liver cancer. Doctors said it was a lifestyle choice, brought on by excessive consumption of alcohol. He killed my grandmother in a car accident that shoulda done him in, instead.'

'I'm so sorry. How did your father take it?'

The man gritted his teeth and tried to hold the lady's eye. 'It drove him to drink, Miss. He couldn't cope with losing his ma, she was everything to him. He... he ended up dying on a trip to Earth-2, got blown from an airlock.'

'An accident?'

'I can't be sure, ma'am. He was very depressed. Drank all the time.'

'I see. Well. Thank you for candor, but I'm very sorry...'

'Victor, ma'am. My name is Victor. Please, ma'am. I never touch the stuff. You can ask the other fellas. I'm a good guy, cook pancakes for 'em when they all get drunk out there mining sludge.'

'Victor, it seems there is a propensity for mental illness and addiction in your blood, perhaps even cancer. You are welcome to work on Juxor for as long as you wish, but I'm afraid we won't be able to help you procreate.'

'Please, you can't make me go back out there! Not with those... *those things!* I'm here for my family. All my mom ever wanted was a grandbaby of her own—not to hold you understand—just to know that he or she is out there among the stars. I know I could have tried on Earth-2, but there's not a lot of work there, and with her debt and the rumors about this place.'

'And what rumors are those?' Farah asked, butting into the conversation.

'That this place is run by women like yourself, beautiful, smart women who are trying to make the best of the men who come here. That if you work here in the sludge and show yourself to be strong and clever they'll take you in to their paradise and for a time you'll live like a king, watching your kids grow in the bellies of a dozen women and helpin' build their Fortress in the storm.' Victor didn't even seem to notice that this new woman was wearing a baggy jumpsuit instead of the flowing white dress of the other woman, or that her hair lay flat and greasy on her head instead of done up in some unnamable pattern like the red-headed woman.

'That's preposterous,' Farah said.

'Indeed,' the woman said, 'there's hardly a man alive worth fathering a child with five of us, let alone a dozen. I'm sorry, sir, your rumors are unfounded.'

'The rumors never said anything about those crab, miss! No one told me that instead of getting to procreate with a half-dozen women I'd watch my friends get eaten alive by some lightning crab that can smell the sludge!

You have to take me in! I can't go back out there, just think of my poor mother. All she wants is a child. And I'm smart, I'm plenty smart. Graduated with honors from Gates University on Earth-2 with a mechanical engineering degree. Ask Kane, ask him! I've improved efficiency ten percent on some of those drills, and stopped the leaks ma'am. With those demons out there nothing is as important as stopping the leaks.'

'There's nothing I can do,' the woman said.

'Yes there is!' the man said and tore the woman's dress away, flimsy thing that it was.

Farah screamed, but the woman didn't bat an eye. Instead, she dropped into a crouch, then popped back up and punched the Victor in the throat. He reeled backwards, gasping for air, but by the time he caught his breathe a teenage boy and girl had run to help. They each seized him by one of his arms and pulled him backwards. Victor struggled. He was far brawnier than the teens, but then the girl savagely kicked him in the back of his calf and he buckled and slipped. When he did, the boy grabbed him by the throat and roughly dragged him backwards. At this point, a third teen sprinted towards the struggle, then opened a plazzglass door that Farah hadn't even realized was there. The ever-present storm of Juxor howled into the calm, quiet hallways, rain wet the stone floor, and wind caught the woman's torn gown and pulled at it angrily. It billowed from her waist, doing nothing to conceal her breasts or her red shock of pubic hair as she approached the man.

'Do you know who you attempt to rape, Victor?'

'I didn't mean to! Please, don't send me back out there with the crabs!'

'I am Iris McKenna, chair of the planetary council of Juxor, though in truth, it matters little who I am, for the punishment would be the same.'

84

'No!' Farah screamed, thinking of the long descent down into the stormy waters below.

Iris turned on Farah with piercing blue eyes—her red hair was tame no longer, whipped about in the wind, the delicate orchids that had been in her tresses were smashed beneath her feet on the slick floor. 'The punishment is the same for any person who dares assault another in such a manner, is it not, children?'

'To violate another is to violate one's self. To violate one's self is to limit one's gift to the universe. The Carbon Man and Mother Ocean have no place for limits on Juxor,' the three teenagers responded in unison. Farah saw that a few other women had made their way towards the ruckus. They stood far enough back that the wind and rain from the storm outside wouldn't dishevel their hair or wet their flowing dresses. Most of them held coy smiles on their lips or murmured the prayer to eager youngsters as they gently held them back from the scene.

'You can't kill him!' Farah pleaded, stepping between the man and McKenna, getting soaked by the rain in the process.

'That is for Mother Ocean to decide,' Iris McKenna said, and with a flick of her wrist, the three teenagers threw Victor from the towering heights down into the roiling sea below. His scream was soon lost to the roar of the wind. Whatever splash his body made was soundless in the storm.

'Mother Ocean's will is done,' Iris said.

'The Carbon Man must face peril if he is to evolve,' the teenagers responded.

The gathered children smiled and applauded.

13

'I've never seen someone with hair like yours,' Jupiter said to Osha.

'Err, thanks. Red hair is a recessive gene, so it's fairly uncommon, I guess. My sister made a point of some of her kids having it by breeding with blonde men.'

'So uncouth, to think something as beautiful as you could come from breeding,' Jupiter said.

'Thank you? I find it appalling that she could even think of breeding for appearance. It's unethical.'

'And what would you hope to have in offspring?'

Osha shrugged, concentrating on flying the ship over the islands, though the AI would do just fine. Jupiter had said that he wanted to go to uncharted areas, that he was looking for something. Osha had reminded him they'd already taken specimens of the crabs, but Jupiter had insisted. He had said that insects in the wild can't be compared to those in captivity. Osha had finally acquiesced to his demands, leaving Ikamon with Kane.

'I don't know. I'd want them to be smart, I guess, compassionate, with a wicked sense of humor,' she laughed. 'You know I've never talked about this with anyone on this planet? Not even my sister, and she believes procreation to be more a higher priority than anyone.'

'What sweet nectar has driven you to share with me?'

'Nothing like that,' Osha said, noticing Jupiter was slowly scooting towards her despite being buckled into his seat. She jiggled the controls and the ship responded by bouncing on its grav generators. Jupiter fumbled and fell back into his seat and grinned.

'It'd be hard to match your cleverness. That is for certain.'

'You sure are charming for a dog.'

Jupiter stuck his tongue out and pretended to pant. 'A dog? I prefer to think of us as butterfly and flower, for you are as irresistible as nectar, the color of your hair far more inviting than the most garish of wildflowers.'

Osha ignored his advances. Despite what Kane had said, she was used to men flirting with her, and usually found it obnoxious. 'I like what you said to Kane. I've tried arguing with him so many times—about how if there's a god it can't logically be benevolent because of all the suffering in the universe, that kind of thing—but he always dismisses me as soon as I start to quote philosophers or scientists. I can't get through to him. My sister and all her little breeders don't want anything to do with me, and most of the men on this planet come just to get rich or get laid.' Osha sighed. 'It's tiring. I guess I agreed to take you on this trip just because you're curious.'

'Would you like to hear a poem?' Roman said, taking a piece of yellowed paper out of his uniform. Osha didn't think she'd ever seen paper outside of a museum or library at the planet's university.

'Uh, sure.'

Roman cleared his throat:

'Through the rain she flew, unflappable,
Flapping her wings, uncappable,
Her mouth that is, which I long to kiss,
To feel her breath upon my lips,

Spread her legs, so I can taste her-'

'That's quite enough!' Osha said, her face bright red. 'Women are not spoken to in such a way on Juxor. And certainly no one writes poems. It wasn't very good anyway,' Osha lied.

'I was hoping it would make you laugh.'

'You already did during your absurd argument with Kane, showing him that a benevolent god doesn't exist.'

'That argument is flawed,' Jupiter said after a moment, hiding behind a wide grin.

'Oh? And how's that?' Osha was much more comfortable getting back to good academic debate. She did not much like what Roman—Jupiter! His name was Jupiter! She did not much like what his poem had done to her.

'Just because bad things happen doesn't mean a god doesn't exist or that it's not benevolent.'

'What kind of a god would let those things happen?' Osha demanded.

'One that doesn't have much power.'

Osha chuckled. 'See, this is why I agreed to go with you. That sort of argument is hilarious! That's just what Kane needs. A reminder that whatever boogie man he and my sister worship is just as fallible as the rest of us.'

'And I am happy you shared your sweet laughter with me. Still, to think something is orchestrating this entire expansion besides us seems a stretch to me, but then when you think about the scale of the universe, truly anything is possible. Even a being we would call a god could exist'

'And yet you don't believe in aliens?' Osha countered.

Jupiter smiled broadly and rubbed his stubbly chin. 'You know, I hadn't thought of it like that before. A fascinating proposition.'

'If you had not introduced yourself by talking about my looks and already mentioned breeding with me, you wouldn't be so bad, Romeo.'

'Please, my name is Roman, not Romeo,' Roman said, blushing.

'Do you truly believe we are capable of stopping the aliens?'

'The hybrids, you mean? Oh yes. Ikamon is most clever, as is officer Relkor, and the captain is nothing short of brilliant. We'll figure out how to stop those things.'

'Do you have a history with her?'

'Relkor? God, no. She's with Ikamon, poor man. Doesn't even see what he tried to do for her here.'

'And what is that?'

Roman grinned. 'The captain and I used to date,' he said, in possibly the clumsiest change of conversation ever.

'Did you?' Osha asked, unable to resist the thought of this dog of a man still working under an ex-girlfriend. 'Why'd you stop?'

'I fell in love with a woman on Bulletar, and stayed behind when Sola had completed her mission. I'm still on probation for abandoning ship, but she thinks that if we do well here, maybe I'll earn a badge and can serve out my time working for her.'

'So your relationship is long gone?'

'I haven't had feelings for her for…' Jupiter ticked on his fingers. 'How long have we known each other?' He grinned madly.

'Mother of the Ocean, as soon as I think I might like you, you go and say something like that. So let me get this straight. You loved the captain, but left her for a woman on a planet, then fell in love with her again, but now you want to get with me?'

'Well, basically yes. You see, you're terribly clever, your hair is intoxicating, and I've never met a woman who holds three doctorates.'

'Still, that's what happened?'

'Well there was a woman on Wholhom, Shay was her name, I believe. When we left there to come here I... sort of might have sent a distress beacon back to her. The captain said I couldn't have, but I think I managed to. But after we left that system I realized we didn't have much in common.'

'Because you fell in love with your captain... again.'

Jupiter looked exasperated. 'Look, I only tell you this because I think if we're going to have anything it should be founded on honesty. I... I don't know why it happens, that's just how it is, OK? It's not easy for me. The only way to move on is to let myself fall in love with who my heart pulls me towards. Right now, that's you. You're all I can think about. I feel bad about the captain, and I know I loved her not long ago, but the same thing always happens with her. She seems fine in space, but then as soon as I get planet side I meet someone and just get swept away! I know it makes me sound a queen bee, mating with any drone that comes along, and yet that's how it is. I am a slave to my instincts, and right now you are lighting up like hidden, ultraviolet markings on a flower, compounding your beauty.'

'So why do you do this then? Wouldn't it be easier just to stay on a planet?'

'That's what I was doing until Sola dragged me back into space in the name of the Institute!' Jupiter's voice was almost cracking. He was really getting quite worked up. He wiped an eye, but even from her position piloting the ship, Osha could see he was working hard to fight back tears. 'I don't want to be this way, but I can't help it! But she was right, I love my work, the challenge to the mind, even it means sacrificing the heart.' He wiped his tears. 'Look there. Land down there. They're why I re-joined the Institute. Do you see them?'

Osha nodded, uncomfortable to be with this man that had been trying to woo her who was now reduced to tears. It was unattractive to see him so vulnerable. How could anyone let themselves look this way in front of the person they were trying to seduce? It was strange, and entirely different than how men on Juxor acted. However, another part of her found his honesty refreshing, his smile charming, and his poetry funny. Osha was confused. She'd never felt this way about a man before.

They landed on the island. Like most of the islands of Juxor it didn't have much save scrubby grass, though Osha noted there were tiny snail shells littered about. Then she saw them, little motes of light, hardly brighter than the faraway cracks of lightning. Fireflies. The island was covered in them.

'This is why I agreed to come back to space,' Jupiter said, his voice growing steadier. He walked forward in a crouch with an open container. He hesitated barely a moment before deftly swooping one out of the air. 'Looks like this variety found a way to consume snails. Not unique, but undoubtedly unusual. I'm sure Ikamon will be very interested,' he said, scribbling something on his tablet as he examined the fireflies. 'It'd be great to find…ah yes, see here? Not much of a flowering plant, but a dandelion is flower, nonetheless. That explains how the adults survive here. It's just like Kane said, we always find what we're looking for,' Roman said, finally smiling again, his little bout of hysterics gone.

Osha was appalled. 'Wait, you actually believe that nonsense? That there's a firefly god just like there's a carbon god?'

'I prefer to think of her as a goddess, but more or less yes, I think something is responsible for these creatures being present on every seeded world, even a stormy one like Juxor. I had previously considered the idea that the force preserving them was a quirk of evolution due to the lights, some sort of algorithm, perhaps, about the distasteful chemical in their guts, but you force me to consider the outlandish idea that, indeed, an alien is responsible. When I speak of a Firefly Goddess, I think that is what I am referring to.'

Osha could almost hear the capital letters. *Mother of the Ocean, is he serious?*

'You're as crazy as Kane! Get in the ship, we're going back to land. And to think I almost considered going on a date with you... you zealot.'

Roman grinned at her, but when she did not return the smile he hung his head and got on the vessel. He spent their flight back scribbling in his notebook. Osha found she didn't really care what about.

14

'Sorry about all that,' Iris McKenna said to Farah, pushing off the wet and tattered remains of her dress, and straightening back up. She extended a hand to Farah, doing nothing to hide her now completely naked body.

'Iris McKenna, a pleasure to meet you, though I would have preferred the situation hadn't been so animated. You are from the *Artemis*, I presume, sent here to solve the crisis that distressed Victor so?'

'You... you killed him,' Farah stammered and the other women in the hallway giggled.

Iris laughed, her freckled breasts heaving as she did. 'Oh hardly. We don't believe in capital punishment on Juxor. Banishment, however, is perfectly just.'

'So you banished him to a rocky coast twenty meters below?'

Iris smiled and put an arm around Farah's shoulder. 'Come dear, observe.' Iris led Farah over to the window. Down below, Victor was just pulling himself out of the ocean onto a craggy shore. Armed guards awaited him and loaded him onto a ship that after a moment took off and headed for the spaceport.

'It was fortuitous, really, that he was so close to a Portal, or else the show would have gone on far longer. I'm glad you didn't have to see all that.'

'What on Earth-4 are you talking about? A show? What I saw bordered on religious insanity. Or will saying such things get me thrown from the Portal too? And put some damn clothes on! What's wrong with you?'

'Officer Relkor,' Iris read the name on Farah's jumpsuit, 'an unsightly name on an unsightly garment. A name given to you by a man, no doubt. Come with me, it has been so long since we've been visited by the Institute. A decade, it seems. Perhaps I can dispel any notions you might have about our planet, and get back to the far more important task of stopping those creatures that are hurting men like poor Victor's friends. Which reminds me: Celia, look into Victor's story. If it's true, pay off the mother's debt and get dear Victor on a ship back to Earth-2. Tell him we'll pay for it if he agrees to the operation. Now, for the third time, come, dear, I have much to show you. Judging by the grass stains on your hideous uniform you are the botanist, and I very much doubt your particular expertise is needed at the moment. Let your men work on our problem while I convince you to leave the rest of our world alone, and get you into something warm.'

Farah's blood boiled at the idea of who *her men* were right now. She looked at the Portal. Yes, perhaps it would be a punishment fitting for those two knuckleheads if they could solve the problem of the planet that they had caused in the first place. She acquiesced, and let the naked woman lead her away from the Portal. This McKenna had the right of it. Farah didn't know what she could do about flesh-eating crabs. Better to distance herself from that disaster, and perhaps make it known who'd really caused it. Mad as she was, it would be unjust to get Cat in trouble for such an incident. Pity the other McKenna wasn't right about the aliens.

'Are you sisters to Osha, by any chance?'

Iris sighed. 'Is it that obvious? Yes I suppose it is, there really aren't many redheads traveling the stars, are there? A recessive gene, you know, often blown out by those of your stock. Our mother was careful to choose for it; both of our fathers had to be pure.'

'Excuse me?'

Iris laughed. 'Oh just something we think about while we do our work, not skin color anymore, thank Darwin, but what sorts of genes we all have. Only one of my children has red hair, the others all beautiful shades of brown and even black, though we're not here to talk about our methods, but what we've achieved.'

Iris steered Farah down into a doorway. Instead of the long, pristine hallway, broken up only by plazzglass windows showing the perpetually raging storm outside, Farah found herself in a room of blooming flowers.

'How did you get orchids out here? It's practically impossible to ship anything that's not a good source of food for people or insects. We don't even have all of these back home on Hot Earth.'

'Indeed.' Iris smiled and plucked one of the flowers, letting it gently caress against her still-naked breast. 'They're difficult to grow, of course, takes fine attention to detail, but then, we have men willing to go to such lengths.'

'Bernard!' Iris called out and a man answered. His arms were burly, his fingers rich with earth. He wiped them off on his pants and smiled as he approached the two women. He, like the other man, was also shirtless. His chest was just as muscled. Ken didn't have a chest like that, Farah thought. Hell, *Roman* didn't have a chest like that. The man was built like an oak tree.

'Iris, darling, what have you done with your *Phalaenopsis*?'

Iris absentmindedly reached for her hair and found that, indeed, the flower was missing. 'A brute threw it out the Portal,' Iris said and winked at Farah.

'Other than that, I find the wardrobe change refreshing,' Bernard said.

'Oh behave, you beast. Bernard fathered my second child, and a few other pups around here. I like his attention to detail, otherwise he'd be back in the sludge, isn't that right, Bernard?'

'We live to serve the Mothers of the Ocean,' he replied with a roguish grin. 'What brings you to the Fortress?'

'Officer Relkor here had a spat with her crew, right, darling? I found her on a walk-about, and was thinking maybe you could tell her a little bit more about our work here.'

'Yeah,' Farah said, trying to keep her eyes off Bernard. It seemed that perhaps he'd picked a cucumber and was storing it for later. 'For starters, why the hell are you walking around naked, and why aren't any of the men wearing shirts?'

Iris and Bernard tittered together. 'They don't let us wear shirts!' Bernard said and laughed some more. He had a refreshing accent. He was probably from one of the Earths if he retained any cultural markers that obvious. Most of the Inner worlds spoke flat English or Chinese. Nobody lived on the Outer Worlds yet.

'Oh, Bernard hush,' she playfully batted his arm. Farah could swear she saw the cucumber move. 'A keen eye to musculature is important. Every woman gets to pick their men, so the males like to preen as nature intended.'

'It is comfortable here, and after a month out there in the rain, living in your slicker and boots, it's wonderful to come inside and be able to work on something besides pumping carbon from the ground,' Bernard said. 'Now, as for Iris, normally she is a bit more modest. I guess being a goddess required a wardrobe change?' Bernard said.

'Well then why on Earth-4 are you still naked?' Farah asked.

'Darling, does it bother you so?' Iris said, rolling her eyes. 'Honestly, you're worse than the men.'

'Iris, you don't know what it's like on the other worlds,' Bernard said, 'Women can't walk around like this without fear of being assaulted verbally, or even physically. If your body is making her uncomfortable, you should change. I don't want you to have to throw her out a Portal.'

'You dare tell a goddess what to do?'

'Even a goddess as beautiful as you can use a silver tongue.'

Iris smiled and Farah found herself thinking that Ken would never say such a thing. He hardly stood up to her, and couldn't mold a compliment without speaking about the ocean in some way.

'Fine, I'll get dressed if I'm making you uncomfortable, but surely you can do the same for me? I can't stand that uniform you're wearing, and besides it's soaking wet from Victor's transgression. Let us get it cleaned for you before you return to your ship.'

'Fine, anything to get those put away.' Farah gestured at Iris's boobs. 'I'm not on duty anyway. I have questions, though, and want them answered. First off, you know Kane is out there preaching to his men that you're some kind of goddess? That if men work they'll get a chance to come here and wallow in all this?'

Iris and Bernard shared a look.

Farah took a deep breath. 'Of course you do. I guess its fine so long as you know he's using your breasts as a carrot to make men work.'

'Yes, darling, of course I do, it was I who put him up to it. Now come along, I think the gardens have done their job, don't you? Let's get me into a little more clothing and you into something more becoming.'

The pair walked down another austere hallway. Farah had to admit, the place was beautiful. The halls were wide and decorated with minimal elegance. Paintings and vases, an exotic delicate plant here and there. The ceilings were tall and made of plazzglass, a constant reminder of the storm raging outside.

'It seems like a different world than out there where the men live.'

'Indeed it is. The mission we gave them is to strengthen this planet by exporting our sludge. Our job is to grow our workforce and the genetic stock of this world.'

'Using yourself as breeders?'

'Who else but women could ever hope to guide evolution? Kane and Dr. Fisk report to us which teams are most efficient, and from those teams we pick strong men with the best education we can find. We give them a month to live here among us, and if in that time, they prove themselves to be intelligent, kind, and know something of their pedigree, then they may breed with one of us, maybe more if we choose.'

'Couldn't you just get them to leave a sample in a cup?'

'You try running a world's economy with masturbation. Not the same motivation as this,' Iris gestured to her still-naked body and laughed. 'But here we are. Come let's get dressed.'

Iris took Farah into a room filled with clothing. It was more fabric than Farah had ever seen outside of her mother and sister's wardrobes back on Earth-4. There were fabrics in every color, styles dating back centuries. It was all *real*. No synthetics. All plant fibers. Farah half-wondered if she'd find actual *silk* among the garments, that's how extravagant the closet was. It couldn't have all been manufactured on Juxor, not without a good crop of cotton or hemp, and neither were listed on Juxor's report. The cost of importing it all boggled Farah's mind. Iris picked out another of the long, flowing dresses she had been wearing earlier, this one a rich purple, and held it over her arm as Farah perused her choices. Finally, she settled on a green dress that flowed as well; it seemed to be the fashion here.

'Excellent choice, and the size looks right too. Now, off with the uniform.'

'Don't you have a changing room?'

'We're in it, darling. Come now, you're not shy about your body in front of a fellow woman, are you?'

'No. But I did not start my day intending to be playing dress up,' Farah grumbled. 'Can't you turn around or something?'

'Is your body that scandalous? I will avert my eyes, but please don't ask me not to peek,' Iris said.

Farah clenched her jaw and threw off her uniform. She would not let this goddess wannabe get the better of her.

'Oh. Wow.'

'I had a date this evening, though that's no longer happening,' Farah said.

'And he expects you to wear this?' Iris said, gesturing at Farah's lingerie. Though really it was far more than what most consider lingerie. Farah had procured the pieces from across the Seeded Worlds. It was all black lace and leather straps. Farah usually felt that she looked as dangerous as she did seductive.

'*I* like to dress this way.'

'Then why are you blushing?'

99

'Because I hadn't expected to be naked in front of an Ocean Goddess this morning! Now turn around, this stuff is wet and I'm not going to wear it under that dress.'

Iris smiled but didn't say anything, only turned around while Farah pushed out of the lingerie. Except it wasn't that easy. Farah could get dressed herself. She found it erotic, really, pulling on leggings, cinching leather garters, putting her pert breasts into brassiere, fantasizing the entire while about Kensei. Even after all these years together he was left speechless when he first saw her on a new planet. He'd tease her about not taking it off while his deft fingers slowly undressed her. Ken would stop talking when he kissed the places on her body that were completely naked. He'd remove a legging, then kiss her toes and calf, remove a garter and kiss the narrow band of skin the leather had been masking. Farah found that her fingers simply weren't as deft as his, they grew clumsy with anger. She wasn't supposed to be here, soaked down to her lingerie, with some nymphomaniac smirking across the closet. She was supposed to be anticipating Kensei's dinner and her dessert for him. His Mango, he still called her, named after what they'd first dined on before they'd made love. But it seemed Ken's dinners were just lies. Lies and danger to the Institute and the Charter she had sworn to uphold. Roman's transgressions, dumb as they were, weren't nearly as dangerous. Beetles could cause famines. They had before, and would again, but they paled in comparison to visions of sea monsters. The idea of Kensei releasing oceanic creatures was stupefying. Squids on Earth-1 could get to be meters long. Even tuna fish were longer than a man. And now a simple crab had caused so much destruction. To think what horrors Kensei might have released into the oceans of inner Seeded Worlds… and *for her*. It was too much. Such reckless disregard for all Farah believed in.

'Relkor, dear, you're shaking.'

'Can you help me get undressed?' Farah threw her hands up in exasperation.

'I thought you'd never ask.'

Farah immediately felt Iris's warm hands on her back as if she'd been waiting a breath away for Farah to ask for her help. She easily moved from strap to strap, taking them off piece by piece so that Farah found her lingerie falling away, until all that was left were her bra and panties. 'You know, with your passion, brilliance, and these perky tits you could be a Mother of the Ocean,' Iris whispered, her breath hot in Farah's ear. 'You could leave whatever man you thought you cared about behind, and live here as a queen. Men would fight to undress you.'

'I'm not interested in *men* right now,' Farah said.

'Oh?' Farah felt Iris's mouth sink into her neck. Her lips sent a shiver down Farah' spine and the way her tongue gyrated slowly made Farah moist between the legs. Farah tried not to focus on how her body was responding, but the truth was she'd been horny all day. Landing on a new planet always did that to her—it was when Ken was at his finest, or rather, *had been.*

'That's quite enough,' Farah said and stepped away from Iris. Her body shuddered as she did, clearly in disagreement.

'Men only touch our Mothers when we say they may. Some of our women go months, even years, without so much as looking at a cock. In those times many of us find other ways to amuse ourselves.'

Farah took the green dress and pulled it on over her bra and panties, worried Iris could smell her excitement. Farah cursed Ken. He did this to her, he was supposed to be the one to take off her lingerie, not this bisexual floozy from an alien world. She shook her head, trying to clear

Iris's kiss from her mind. Her body did not seem to want to forget. Farah tried to cover the feeling with bluster.

'So this is how you live? You amuse yourselves here in exchange for growing babies and the men are left out there to face those freaky crabs and dream of spending a night with you? You live a life of pleasure while they risk their lives.'

Iris shrugged and stepped back from Farah and began to dress herself. While Farah yanked her dress on with the same graceless effort she used to don her uniform, Iris slid into hers with practiced elegance. Farah rolled her eyes. She was in no way a lesbian. Her Captain, her mom, and her sisters were the only women she'd ever loved, and yet this woman made everything seem so goddamn sexy. Farah turned away as Iris finished pulling the dress over her large, freckled breasts. Farah tried not to think that she would forever remember what it felt like to have those breasts pushed against her.

'The problem you are here to solve makes our way of life seem barbaric. Those creatures are grotesque, and I sincerely hope that despite whatever wrongs the men of your ship have done to you, they can solve this problem. But in truth, it was always a dangerous job. The weather here can turn from foul to fatal in a heartbeat. We lose men to the tide or to the work often. They know this coming in, and we pay their families or friends back on their home worlds for their losses. We'd use machines, but there are human beings willing, and it would cost a fortune to import the iron we'd need to build a fleet, and we'd rather not deal with the Corps. I know it's cruel, but in a way, it's another hand of evolution. The men who come here have no place on any of the Seeded Worlds. Can you imagine? Five Earths to choose from—or truly four that are inhabitable, I suppose—and the other dozen Inner worlds all growing rapaciously and in need of people, and yet not feeling as if you had a place on any of them? Not belonging to a planet, but wandering forever, never finding a home, never having a family or being able to watch those your love grow old.'

Farah didn't find it very hard to imagine. She hadn't stayed on a planet for more than a month since her days in school. She visited her family on Hot Earth when she could, but it was far less than once a standard year.

'We give those men a chance at a dream. Some, like sweet Bernard, come to live with us year round. Others find they like the work and become our project leads or engineers. Still others make their money, spread their seed, and return home wealthier than when they left. Some never return, and this is tragic, but it is the way of things. This planet is the forefront of human evolution. We are choosing the best and the oceans are eliminating those who could find a home nowhere else. It is harsh, but then evolution always is. While you stay here I ask you take leave from your ship and learn about us, so a woman of the Institute will know what it is we do here.'

'Well that shouldn't be a problem, I quit.'

'Oh?' Iris's eyes gleamed. 'Well in that case, perhaps you'd like to stay with us? Bernard can get your things and you're more than welcome here.'

'All I have to do is give my uterus over, right?'

Iris laughed. 'Not all of us fulfill that calling. My sister, for example, is notably deficient. There are roles here for you besides that, though. Come, meet the others and see for yourself.'

Farah found herself agreeing. She didn't know if she'd stay on this crazy place, but something about it, something about the idea of being able to throw a man she didn't like from a Portal, appealed to her. Besides, she knew that Ken and Jupiter weren't going to solve the crab crisis overnight.

'I'll sleep here tonight.'

'Excellent, let me find you a dinner date, male or female?'

'I don't think I want a date like that, how about mixed company?' Farah said, hoping she'd picked the safest option.

Iris smiled. 'Oh, you're going to enjoy your time here quite a bit I think.'

15

The crab clamored back and forth inside of the plazzglass cube. It had ceased spinning its webs. It had ceased doing anything except for walking back and forth, clicking its diamond-tipped claws occasionally. Kensei found himself empathizing with the creature. Like it, he was trapped in a room he didn't wish to be in, and like it, he had no idea what he was supposed to do.

'I thought the Institute was supposed to be chock full of brilliant scientists?' Osha McKenna said.

'You're not among our ranks and seem to be the most brilliant butterfly this planet has created,' Roman said.

'Mother of the Ocean give it a rest. You haven't met anyone except for that demagogue, Kane.'

'I've met you and I feel that is already quite enough. Does the first sip the mason bee takes after emerging from it pupa taste less sweet? No I say, no! A flower that blooms despite such prickly surroundings is all the more beautiful and attracts bees like no other.'

McKenna rolled her eyes and suppressed a smile. No one talked in metaphors on Juxor. No one threw poetry into conversation as easily as this man.

'Please, Roman, we must solve this quickly so when the captain returns with Farah she will not still be so angry at me,' Kensei said, wringing his hands. He was unsure of how to proceed, and was happy to brainstorm with the two scientists. Truly, he didn't know what else to do. It was hard to think about anything when he knew Farah was so mad. Normally she reserved such rage for Roman, and now Kensei was hoping the entomologist would help him win his wife back. Even after so many years of marriage, love was difficult for Kensei.

'Ikamon, it's not your fault. These things are in no way related to a snow crab. It's a case of convergent evolution,' Roman said. 'You see, darling Osha, poor Ikamon released a tasty treat for his love and received only scorn. I hope you find the lunar moths of Guadalupe far more beautiful. They, like me, have no desire save to be with she who lights their heart more brightly than the moon. I suppose I should count myself lucky that I can speak to you at all, for the moths I released on Guadalupe have no mouths.'

McKenna took a deep breath. It looked like she was trying to ignore this Roman Jupiter. It was not working. Kensei had seen Roman seduce enough women to know when it was probably going to work. Kensei sighed. Roman could get a different woman on every planet, yet Kensei had to work so hard just to hang on to his precious Mango.

'These alien "crabs" as Kane calls them, either used our DNA as a blueprint, or something designed them to look this way. It's the only explanation that is logical. I've been studying them, and I find it highly unlikely that the radiation of our sun is strong enough to create such extreme mutations in such a short amount of time. I've already shown you their diamond claws and carbon filament web, but they also seem to arrive with thunderstorms, indicating some sort of electromagnetic sensory organ, or even more interesting, perhaps an ability to store electrical charges. You are correct that they have similarities to the moths because of the webs but, you have no proof of the dragonfly metamorphosis. We don't know for certain that these are the nymph stage of that creature, and besides, nothing on Earth-1 used electricity to hunt,' McKenna said.

'There were eels that did. They could create an electric pulse that would stun fish. Sharks, too, could sense electromagnetic fields. Though neither of those creatures have been released here on Juxor, at least not to my knowledge,' Ikamon said gloomily.

'I'm running a DNA analysis between the crabs, the moths, and the dragonflies as we speak, but even if it does prove to be hybridized, how do you explain the arrangements of carbon they use and the electromagnetic disturbances?' McKenna said.

Roman grinned and looked from McKenna to Kensei. 'She makes good points, brilliantly argued. Like the honeybee confronted with a dandelion, I find her hard to resist. What if she's right?'

'I would love to discuss your theories on the hidden alien conspiracy in detail, but it does not affect our situation. We cannot prove that these hybrid crabs are aliens, and if we did, so what? They would still exist and would still be destroying your carbon reserves and eating people. How the creatures came to be is irrelevant. What we must do is figure out how to use them,' Kensei said.

'Use them? They're monsters! Even before they started killing people they weren't anything but a pestilence.'

Roman scratched his stubbly chin and approached the crab, which was still pacing back and forth in its enclosure. 'My butterfly, I hate to disagree with you, but Ikamon has a point. These things are far more efficient at gathering carbon than pumps. Didn't I read that the reserves they get into are totally cleaned out?'

'Yes, but they turn it into more of themselves.'

'That might not be a bad thing, you know?' Kensei said, rubbing his head. 'How do most people use your carbon?'

'Mostly for plastics, or they make graphite as a lubricant, diamonds for computers or batteries, and some use it as fertilizers.'

'So, few people use it in its raw form?'

'Not really. It has to be refined. It's not like its crude oil. It has a lot of impurities. What factories we do have here are devoted to purifying the sludge, and then we export it either as a liquid or powder.'

'These creatures convert it into a variety of forms. Their shells are almost pure carbon nanostructures, while the webs they make are long chains of it. Perhaps we have been thinking of them in the wrong way. They are little carbon refineries, you know? Little factories that take a crude form of the element, and join it together into more complex molecules. This may represent the most significant discovery of how creatures use carbon since plants learned how to make sugar,' Ikamon said, warming up to the idea.

'You're forgetting one thing: they kill people if we get near them,' McKenna said. 'Even if we could harvest them, or whatever it is you are proposing, how would we do it without risking lives? Kane and my sister might have no moral qualms with such actions, but I do. If those crabs so much as smell sludge on a slicker it activates some part of their brain and turns them into feeding machines.'

'You're brilliant!' Roman said, then ran out of the lab and into the hallway. He returned a minute later with a rain slicker and a pair of boots, both covered in the carbon sludge. 'Open the box!'

'What are you, crazy?' McKenna said, but Ikamon obliged. He could feel where this was going. They might be able to solve this after all. Farah might still forgive him!

The little crab perked up immediately and tried furiously to climb the slick plazzglass walls of its enclosure, attempting to get at the source of carbon. Roman dropped the slicker in and the crab began to devour it, sucking up the sludge and spinning a web.

'What are you doing?'

'It's not efficient because they normally work in groups, but with enough food, it should get there,' Roman said, watching the crab work. Sure enough, after a few minutes it had completed its web and nestled itself inside. 'All right, give it a few hours and let's watch what happens.'

So they did. They watched and watched as the crab did nothing at all for hours. It just sat there, completely inert, in its cocoon of web.

While they waited, Roman recited two sonnets and a couple of haikus to Osha. Kensei deeply regretted showing him the form of poetry. Much as he tried, he simply could not appreciate Roman's poetry, be it:

Sharp orange butterfly
Flying in the field of my heart
Pollinate me please.

or

Delicate blossom
Grown in thunderstorm's tumult
You are so gorgeous

Ikamon shuddered each time Roman finished scribbling in his yellowed notepad. How he wished he could be with Farah right now, discussing all that they'd learned over a dinner of fresh-cut tuna or those damn snow crabs he'd released.

McKenna's reaction to Roman's poetry didn't make Kensei feel any better. Though she openly told Roman she did not care one way or the other about the poems devoted to her, she listened intently to each one. It seemed that whoever taught poetry on Juxor focused more on appreciation than criticism.

Eventually, though, Roman tired of writing poetry and turned the conversation back from McKenna to her work. 'Tell me, do you ever return to the sights?'

'Yes, we normally do after a day or two, and find the things all gone.'

'And there's no surveillance?'

'No. Any cameras we leave are destroyed. It's like they can eat electricity.'

'Interesting hypothesis. Let's test it.' Roman grabbed the crate and hurried out of the lab, Ikamon and McKenna at his heels.

They caught up to him down by the shore, the box open, a butterfly net in his hand.

'It's happening,' he said with a mad look in his eyes. 'They *must* be sensitive to electromagnetic fields. I think all the tech in your lab was distracting it, but that storm should set it straight.' Roman pointed to a big angry thunderhead on the horizon.

Still the creature did nothing.

'Ikamon, do you have your badge on you?'

'*Hai*, of course.'

'Give it to me.'

Kensei passed Roman the badge that showed his rank as second officer of the Institute. Roman tossed it into the ocean. 'I left mine in the lab. I bet it's messing up the thing's biometrics. Sweet Osha, do you have anything that uses electricity besides that brilliant brain of yours?'

McKenna nodded, but ignored Roman's outstretched hand. She climbed back up the ladder to the deck and put her radio down on the carbon composite planks. It was lucky the creatures only seemed to like the sludge, she thought as she made her way back down the ladder and along the craggy shore. Pretty much everything on Juxor was made of carbon. The shelters of the workers, their rain slickers, even Osha's lab largely used carbon composites and plastics derived from the sludge. It was just so much easier than importing metal or wood. By the time she returned, the mass of webbing had started to pulsate. It looked like a heartbeat at first, illuminated by flashes of lightning from the approaching storm. The webbing split and a white mass was revealed within. Slowly it emerged. Six thin, hairy legs pushed forth a large head with compound eyes and no mouth. Then the creature's long body emerged. Osha thought it would never end. It was well over fifteen centimeters from eye to tail. The creature stood there for a moment, then began to inflate its wings — they were long, almost 30 centimeters across — and slowly changed from some kind of mushy looking material to something more like paper covered in a fine fuzz. The creature's exoskeleton changed too. It started a milky white, but as the insect took in more air it grew darker and darker until the scientists were faced with a dark, blue creature with flecks of white the same color as the angry waters splashing at the shore. All and all the creature seemed a perfect mix of moth and dragonfly. After a few minutes it tentatively shook its wings and, finding them sturdy, took to the air. Osha found that she wasn't surprised at all that no one had ever seen it before. Out over the ocean it would vanish, camouflaged perfectly with the choppy sea.

'I can't believe it, you were right,' Osha said.

Roman watched the entire spectacle in awed silence, as a grandmother would watch her child give birth. As soon as the dragonfly moth hybrid began to fly he swung his net down with such ferocity that both Kensei and McKenna gasped.

'Gotchya, you little bastard!' Roman said gleefully. 'It was just waiting for the right conditions. I think your hypothesis about the lightning is a good one. Come on, let's dissect it.'

'Shouldn't we return to the lab?' McKenna said.

Kensei was amazed and thankful that Roman had been right. The crabs weren't crabs at all! They were mutant dragonfly moths! Kensei had never been so happy. Farah would forgive him! They could have that dinner after all! *All I must do now is save this planet from these strange animals.* A sobering thought. 'Mm... if it is sensitive to electromagnetic fields, that may induce unwanted effects,' Kensei said, and smiled at Roman in thanks.

Roman, though, apparently had never doubted his own expertise on the insect and had already removed a knife from the belt on his uniform and was very carefully slicing open the creature. 'Darwin these things are tough. It's almost impossible to get through unless I follow these seams that hold together its...I don't know if it is a carapace or a thorax...ah, there we go!' Jupiter popped open its end and found a clutch of eggs.

'Unfertilized, no doubt,' Roman said and tossed the sack into his plazzglass cube. He scanned the rest of the creature. 'Definitely *looks* like a dragonfly, but its mouth is atrophied. Wild, huh? And the wings have moth scales. Strange stuff.'

'You still think this thing's not an alien?' Osha said.

'You still think it is?' Roman said. Kensei recognized the hesitation in his voice. He was thankful Roman could at least express countering ideas to the woman he was currently obsessing over.

'It is not important now. We must figure out how to stop them from hurting people. They must return to some breeding ground to fertilize the eggs, then they die,' Ikamon said.

'This is amazing! So all we need to do is find their island, then gather up all of their tiny eggs and smash them,' McKenna said.

'That would certainly be effective, though it may be difficult if the creatures truly are sensitive to electricity,' Kensei said. Lightning flashed and thunder echoed a moment later. It seemed the storm had moved closer. The light drizzle that seemed ever present on Juxor turned into a heavier rain.

'Once there, we'll have to decide if we want to catch the adults before they land, or let them lay the eggs and die so we can harvest their bodies. Either way, some are bound to get through,' Roman had to holler to be heard as the wind picked up.

'Still, you've given us somewhere to start. Thank you, gentlemen, I never thought I'd be saying this, but thank you. Now let's get inside, this storm looks severe. We normally don't get ones like this near the skylift.'

'Our job is not over yet. But come, we must tell the captain of what we've discovered,' Kensei said, shielding his eyes from the driving rain and daring to hope that they could outsmart a bug.

16

It was immediately apparent to Kensei that they had not outsmarted the bugs at all.

A few hundred meters away down the dock the creatures emerged from the sea en masse. Thousands of them, hundreds of thousands, boiled out of the ocean and bubbled up the shore line. In the brief flashes of lightning it was impossible to see the creatures individually, only the writhing horde. Kensei jumped back as something scurried over his leg. More of the hybrids were coming out of the ocean around them. Their population had been multiplying.

'Why are they here?' Roman asked.

'This entire facility is made of carbon. Our clothes, our buildings, even the skylift!' Osha said.

'Our clothes are made of hemp, not plastic. We should be fine, but you could be in danger! Quickly, strip down!' Roman said to Osha and eyed her hungrily.

'I am not disrobing,' Osha glared at him.

'I don't think they are interested in us right now,' Kensei said, watching the crabs move towards the spaceport.

'The skylift,' Osha said. 'They've sensed the skylift. That cable is over 100,000 kilometers of carbon nanofibers. The climber that goes up it has a huge carbon battery as well. They're going to destroy it.' She shrieked as another crab pinched at her plastic boots.

Roman hoisted the redhead into his arms.

'Put me down!'

'Ikamon, we have to contact the captain before we lose power. Where's your comm?'

'You threw it in the ocean!'

'Right. Well, let's go for higher ground!'

Kensei nodded and scrambled back up the ladder. Roman followed with Osha over his shoulder, his brawny frame making easy work of the rungs despite Osha's added weight.

In the few seconds it took Kensei to scale the ladder up from the sea, the hybrids engulfed hundreds of meters of the Skylift. The crabs swarmed around it and piled on top of each other, making a mass meters tall. Those that could reach the thin cable grabbed it and climbed and climbed. Already, the greyish tape was blotchy with the black specks of the crab's body. The first station, some three kilometers up, would already be overwhelmed with the crabs. This thin string that connected the surface to outer space was being eaten by the hybrids like a spaghetti noodle.

A siren blared and red lights flashed. People poured out of the squat buildings that made up the spaceport and ran towards the crabs.

'Protect the cable!' Kane's voice boomed over the speakers. The sound of projectile weapons echoed out. Kane must have paid top dollar for the few he had, though they did little good. Each slug of metal could only kill one crab. Still, they did far better than the electrically charged tasers other men wielded. They rushed at the crabs, only to watch the blue light surrounding their weapon fade to nothing. Men bravely beat and hacked at the crabs until the creatures noticed, turned on the men, and consumed

115

them in a mass of dark, sparkling bodies. Transport vessels lifted off laden with men, all the while the crabs climbed higher and higher on the tether that anchored the space station up above.

'There's an *Arrow!*' Roman shouted and Kensei saw it. He fumbled at his belt and pulled out a flare gun. The thing was designed to be used in an oxygen-less environment—rain should be no bother. He fired it into the sky. The *Arrow* turned around and swooped down towards Jupiter, Ikamon, and McKenna who was still struggling in Roman's arms, though she stopped when she saw what the creatures were doing to the skylift.

The *Arrow* came down and rested on its gravity generators a meter above the ocean. 'Get in!' Mondragon yelled.

Ikamon jumped the gap and turned around to catch McKenna as Roman hurled her across the void. She didn't even scream. Her attention was focused elsewhere. Roman jumped in after her and tossed the hybrids that had been attacking her boots off the vessel. Kensei ran to the cockpit. Catalina sat at the controls, her teeth gritted. Kane and Dr. Fisk were there too.

'Where is Farah?' Kensei demanded

'I was hoping you knew,' Catalina said.

'She's at The Fortress,' Dr. Fisk said.

'That is classified information and these *grass-seeders* have no right to know it!' Kane said.

'Where is that?' Mondragon asked, ignoring Kane.

Fisk pointed.

A few hundred meters across the sea was a thrust of buildings nestled in behind a cliff face. The Fortress. It was beautiful, gleaming white, and glass. Even from this distance Kensei could see it was filled with orchards and life, a place of beauty on this dreary world.

There was a terrible sound of rending material as the skylift tore free of its base, taking the crabs with it. Ikamon knew that a skylift wasn't actually supported at the base. Instead, the interita of the station up in space, past geosynchronous orbit, kept the thread taught as climbers moved up and down it. Knowing this made it no less unsettling to see the thin tether break from the ground and then float across the bay, suspended by an anchor hidden kilometers above them, well past the thunderstorms and outside the atmosphere of Juxor. Worse, though, was that it carried the crabs with it. Rockets fired at the second station on the cable, kilometers above the surface, barely above where the crabs had reached. Small rockets directed the cable away from the spaceport to crash down into the ocean as the rest of the skylift lifted up to be reattached. It was a standard safety protocol for the giant structures. Nobody wanted kilometers of the carbon nanofiber, light as it was, to smash into them, so in an emergency most skylifts would jettison the damaged part and salvage the rest of the cable. But these safety protocols failed to anticipate thousands of ravenous lifeforms hungry for its carbon. There was an explosion of bug guts and the cable twisted, then broke free. The bottom few kilometers, covered in the black crabs, multiplying the skylift's weight thousands of times, began to fall onto the Fortress.

17

The ambiance was romantic, the food exquisite, and the company grew more pleasant with each glass of wine.

'So the whole religion thing is a sham?' Farah giggled.

Bernard laughed, his lace-up shirt stretched tight across his chest and arms. Iris smiled. 'Not a sham, darling. Kane certainly believes it, but most of us do not. It's true, in a way, that this universe was made to be tilled. Water and carbon the tinder, you see, and life the match. I find this a terribly romantic notion. I don't know much about the idea of us as goddesses.'

'You love that that is how the men think of you!' Bernard said.

'I was going to say we don't dispel the notion, either.' Iris smiled and sipped her wine. Apparently the grapes grew inside the Fortress. Farah hadn't ever tasted wine so good anywhere besides her home world, Hot Earth.

'Isn't it risky, men living out there, growing more ignorant rather than more aware?'

'We scoop up the smart ones.'

Farah didn't really like what that implied, that the less intelligent were left out on the craggy shores of Juxor, but then, she wasn't sure if that was wrong either. The men knew what they were getting into when they came here. Hard work in exchange for wealth, plain and simple.

If some men were more motivated by the rumors then that was another thing…except Kane made them more than rumors. 'Whether you want to be a goddess or not, Kane has turned you into one.'

Iris smiled and shrugged. 'We are growing a world because of it.'

Farah tried to pay attention to what else Iris was saying, but it was very difficult as one of their feet began slowly rubbing up against her leg. Neither Bernard nor Iris made the slightest indication that it was them. Farah didn't even have the heart to fight it. Her time here had been wonderful. Iris treated her as an equal instead of an insubordinate, as Cat had been prone to do. Instead of just her husband, *all* the men were pleasant and respectful, well, those that weren't thrown from the Portal, but Farah had only seen the one bizarre ritual. Best of all was the food. The food was amazing. Already she'd had a delicate tomato soup that must have been from some heirloom variety, lovely braised carrots dressed with vinaigrette that Iris assured her was produced on Juxor, and a salad with more varieties of greens than the Institute had in their records. When the main course came the fish was a tad overcooked for Farah's taste, but delicious nonetheless. She almost found herself missing Ken, but shook her head out of it. He would have enjoyed the meal, but all he was to her was a lie and a problem.

'Are these Brussel sprouts?' Farah asked, eyeing the plate their server had brought them.

'Grown here on Juxor. We have extensive gardens in the middle of The Fortress. We can give you any vegetable you like.'

'Seeds would be much appreciated.'

Bernard sighed.

'What is it, Bernard?'

'I thought that maybe Ms. Farah would wish to stay, but I see she is still stuck on her skinny little man who doesn't cook his food.'

'Don't be so pushy, Bernard. She's part of a renowned crew of...farmers? What is it exactly that you do out there anyway? Make sure the bugs don't eat too much grass?'

'Ecological management is far more complex than that,' Farah said.

'Isn't it just dumping eggs in the sea and waiting for it all to even out?' Bernard said.

'That's what many thought in the early days. And certainly, the first twenty to forty years of life on most of the Seeded Worlds were marked by boom and bust ecologies. Thousands of flies one day that'd be replaced by thousands of spiders the next. Violent, wild ecosystems unlike anything to ever exist on Earth-1. This went on until the biomass began to build up on these worlds. Once there was enough soil, populations started to equalize, then when the first Interstellar Ecologists got out there they released things they thought would stabilize the ecosystems, sometimes with hilarious or disastrous results.' Farah laughed. She was warming up to her favorite conversation, historical interstellar botany. Bernard and Iris listened intently. Whichever was stroking her leg was moving higher up, towards her knee, then past it. The wine made Farah all the more aware of how delicious it all felt. Ken only ever brewed beer.

'I'm sorry, Farah, you're ah...crackling.'

'Oh is it?' Farah said and looked down at her first officer Badge. It was the only one she had bothered to keep on. She simply couldn't part with it. She had pinned it inside one of the folds of her green dress. Hidden from sight, but, like her black, lacy thong, a reminder of who she was and what had brought her here.

'Excuse me,' she said and leaned into the badge and tapped it to amplify the volume.

'Farah… are you?' Static crackled and made Catalina's voice garbled and hard to understand. 'Breeding faster… thought we had… sky is…falling! Sky… falling!'

Then the comm went dead. Farah looked up at her companions and tried to smile.

'Is this some kind of joke?' Bernard said, his smile shaken.

'Surely your boss respects your time off?' Isis said.

'Of course, she does! Well, not really. Do you normally have communication issues here?' Farah said, fidgeting with her comm.

'All the time, darling, an effect of the storms, oh look, a thick one is rolling in.' Iris nodded to a dark cloud racing towards the plazzglass roof. 'Best thing to do in a storm like this is get in bed and find a way to be distracted, am I right, Bernard?'

'It looks more like a tornado,' Farah began as she stood up and walked towards one of the windows.

There was a huge mass of darkness in the sky coming towards them that seemed to taper down into a nearly invisible thread. The cloud began to pelt the building. Only it was no cloud, it was thousands of the crabs. They fell into the plazzglass roof, plinking so loudly that some of the people in restaurant froze and others stood up. First it was dozens, then hundreds, soon they could no longer see the sky, there were so many crabs clambering about the plazzglass ceiling. Then something smashed into the building with horrible force. The plazzglass celling didn't break, but a horrible crack spread across the roof of the restaurant. It started where the cloud had come from and went on and on.

Farah realized Catalina had been talking about the skylift. The crabs had somehow severed it from its moorings and were now devouring the thing. They were hideously gyrating their bodies in frantic copulation.

'What is this?' Iris shouted.

'This is what ecological engineers solve. I need to get back to my ship. Captain, first officer reapplying for duty,' Farah said, slapping her badge hidden in the folds of her dress. Nothing happened. 'Why isn't my comm working?'

'My sister says those things interfere with wireless communications. Come on, we have a landline.'

They rushed through the building, hordes of screaming women, children, and shirtless men making way into bunkers dug into the rock beneath them.

'Those things can't get through, right?' Iris asked.

'I have no idea. You've been wining and dining me when I should have been working. Darwin, I haven't even heard Ken's theory on how to stop them!' Farah's heart throbbed at the thought of her husband. Catalina had called her to tell her it wasn't the snow crabs Kensei had released a decade ago, but some never-before-seen hybrid, but Farah hadn't wanted to listen. She had told Cat to call her when they were leaving, or if any unregistered plants started killing people. If the crabs were this bad then surely Ken... No, she couldn't think that way, not yet. She had to help these people.

They reached the phone and Iris dialed a number. Farah didn't remember the last time she'd seen tech that old. Living conditions on the inhabited world really did vary widely.

Kane's voice answered. 'Your majesty. Thank the Carbon Man you're alive. We don't have much time. McKenna was right. These things can sense electricity. They'll probably take out the satellite relay for my phone soon.'

'I'm here with Farah Relkor from the *Artemis*. Have you seen her crew?'

There was a shuffling sound and then Kensei's voice came over the radio. 'Farah! Tell me you're OK.'

'I'm fine, Ken! But it looks like your little meal wants to eat us for dinner.'

'They're not crabs, but some kind of bug that feeds on carbon. They will be capable of flight soon.'

So Catalina had been right.

'Jupiter.' Farah scowled.

'We don't have time, my Mango. They are transforming.'

Farah saw that it was true. All along the glass ceiling the disgusting creatures were chewing apart the skylift cable and spinning black webbing that was blotting out the sky. Soon the entire Fortress would be covered.

'They will probably short out the electricity soon. We will get you out when they complete their metamorphosis and leave for the next carbon reserve.'

'We're sitting on our next carbon reserve,' Iris mumbled.

'You get that, Ken? They're not going anywhere.'

'We don't know what to do,' Kensei said.

'Destroy their breeding ground, like you did for those starfish on Tenagra.'

'We can't use anything with electricity!'

Farah's mind spun, her eyes fell upon Bernard's muscled torso.

'Use the men of this world! They can do it. Say it's some kind of ritual feast or something. That the Mothers of the Ocean will be there.'

'We can't risk our lives like that!' Iris hissed.

'If you don't we're already lost. Ken, did you hear me? You have to get the men to help, they'll do it if they know the Mothers of the Ocean will be there!'

But the line was already dead.

Above them, the crabs, or hybrids, or whatever they were, began extruding long threads of black silk out of their bodies. They walked back and forth over the plazzglass, making Farah feel like she was inside some hideous cocoon. The creatures, glutted on their nearby feast of carbon sludge, were already molting. Exoskeletons split open to reveal soft, fleshy versions of the same creatures that then consumed their discarded bodies and began to harden. Farah couldn't be certain, but they had maybe a few molts to go before the things were full grown. That could mean a day or two, or merely hours. The skylift was big enough that not even this mass of creatures was enough to completely consume it, but that only meant they'd come right back here as soon as the next generation of nymphs was large enough.

'Come on, we have to get everyone somewhere safe,' Farah was able to say before the electricity went out and everything went dark. The only light came from the lightning flashing through the threads of black silk, but after a time even that was blocked out. The cocoon was complete, and the Fortress was trapped inside.

18

Though Catalina flew the *Arrow* between thunderheads and lighting strikes with speed and grace not rivaled by many save Fin back at the top of the skylift in the *Artemis,* she couldn't get close enough. Anytime she approached the Fortress her systems blared red, circuit failure.

'What's our plan?' Captain Mondragon demanded.

'We can attempt to create an electromagnetic field to interfere with their molting process if we can find where they nest,' Ikamon said.

'What if they don't nest anywhere?' Roman said.

A chilling thought.

'Some insects just consume and breed without stopping if there's a supply of food. It could take generations of the hybrids to eat that Fortress.'

'We... we are not the Carbon Man,' Kane said.

'Finally, an astute observation,' McKenna said. Catalina had been working with Kane to gather up any crews that were still out working when the crabs had appeared at the skylift.

'The Carbon Man has chosen a stronger warrior,' Kane said, then rushed forward and struck Catalina on the side of the head. She reeled from the blow and Kane seized the controls and tried to steer the ship towards the Fortress.

Roman and Ikamon grabbed him and wrestled him to the back of the ship.

'Don't you see? Carbon has chosen another! We are but pawns to be sacrificed. A failed branch of evolution. These things were its true goal. We must give them our ship. We must!'

There was a dull thud as McKenna struck him across the head with the butt of a flare gun. 'I've waited so long to do that.'

Catalina took the controls and flew the ship away from the Fortress as Ikamon and Roman bound Kane.

'Captain, it is likely that the creatures will not leave this area until all of the resources are gone,' Ikamon said.

'Our reserves our hidden beneath the Fortress,' McKenna said. 'Oceans of sludge. If the creatures are able to sense the existence of that reserve they will stop at nothing to get it.'

'Maybe we can lure them somewhere else?' Roman said.

'There's nowhere,' Kane said, coming to and laughing in between grunts. 'We'll have to bomb the building,' Kane said.

'You'll kill everyone inside!' McKenna said.

'It's them or carbon life on the other planets. You're right, though,' he said, his head lolling about as he weakly struggled at the harness Roman and Kensei had strapped him down in, 'we should let them have their way. They are more powerful than us. The Carbon Man has sculpted a finer weapon than man.'

'Farah is in there.'

'So is my sister.'

'There is no other way. We have no source of carbon that large,' Kane said, grinning. 'We should surrender ourselves to them. Carbon's finest warrior. A bug.'

'What is that?' Roman asked.

'I thought you studied the damn things!' Kane said, growing furious.

'No, that!' Roman said, pointing to a brick building that lay some distance inland of the Fortress.

'The refinery! Roman, you're brilliant' McKenna said and kissed him on the cheek, blushing fiercely as she did. 'That's where we make the sludge into products. There's not as much carbon there as we have in the reserves, but there's a lot. Maybe we could lure them there?'

'What is the refinery like?' Ikamon asked.

'It's a big, brick building, plazzglass windows for light. Lots of tanks and pipes,' McKenna said.

'We need all of the men there as soon as we can,' Kensei said, 'the fishermen too. Captain, get clear of this and radio for everyone to meet offshore on the far end of the island. Tell them to bring their nets. I have a plan.'

'What kind of plan?'

Kensei's eyes twinkled, 'Crab-boil, you know?'

'Wait a minute, wait a minute, hold on just a minute,' Roman said. Everyone looked at him. 'You guys saw that, right? Osha totally just kissed me!'

19

It was as Roman had predicted, the diamondcrabs' behavior changed in the presence of so much food. The crabs wouldn't leave their feast. They just kept feeding, molting, and becoming adults which would fly around the Fortress in a big cloud of insects that would breed and then fall into the ocean or sometimes the decks of the assembled fishing ships. The thunderstorm would not dissipate—it seemed there were enough of the creatures to attract the storm, either that or bad luck and worse weather was conspiring against the people of Juxor. Fortunately, though, the diamondcrabs still seemed to display some kind of group behavior, for none of them attacked the ships, even though they were made from carbon composites nearly identical to the Fortress. Kensei's plan rested solely on his understanding of this behavior. He wished he had a god to pray to, but he didn't, only his grandmother to ask for guidance. Even if he failed and was eaten by the diamondcrabs, he hoped she'd be proud.

As soon as the ships had brought around a hundred men, Kensei demanded they act. No one argued, no one wanted to see the Fortress get eaten any further. Captain Mondragon didn't like the plan, but without any other idea she'd agreed to it. She piloted an *Arrow* behind the far shores of the island that would determine the fate of Juxor. She'd had three more of the transport vessels sent down, just in case. They were slaved to her console. Normally Fin could pilot them remotely, though the thunderstorm growing above the diamondcrabs made both visual and radio contact impossible. If Kensei's plan didn't work, plan B was desperate. Captain Mondragon would bring the Arrows as close as she could without the electromagnetic interference knocking them offline so the men of Juxor could escape. They'd have to swim to the transport vessels. Kensei hoped that the crabs didn't have other ways of locomotion he and Roman had overlooked. They hadn't seen any fins or webbing on the crabs, but it seemed the pace of evolution was quickening on the Seeded Worlds. Kensei half-worried the crabs would mutate before their very eyes. But enough of that. Their backup plan wasn't any good. They'd have to be successful if Farah was to come back aboard the *Artemis* and Kensei was to have his Mango back.

'Open the tanks!' Kensei cried as the crabs went about eating the Fortress. Men inside the refinery opened up huge vats of sludge and began spreading it across the floor. The diamondcrabs ignored it. If anything, the scent of if sent the diamondcrabs into a fervor. They gobbled up the Fortress with renewed vigor, scrambling clear of the plazzglass windows and attacking the carbon composite frame of the structure.

It was then that Kensei saw her through the plazzglass windows. Farah Relkor, love of his life. She was wearing a green dress and standing resolutely between the diamondcrabs and a mob of women and children. Big, muscled men, shirtless and far brawnier than Kensei would ever be, cowered behind this thin rail of a women. Farah clenched her fists, daring the diamondcrabs to break through.

129

'It's not working!' a man yelled from outside the Fortress and ran forward, beating at the crabs mercilessly with a length of metal. He was a hulking man, much bigger than Kensei, but the diamondcrabs were not intimidated. They turned on him, sensing his grungy clothes, perhaps, or the slick, greasy carbon deposits in his hair and devoured him as he uselessly tried to fight off the monsters. Ikamon had heard stories of the piranha, a fish that could supposedly strip flesh from the bones of a man in minutes. These diamondcrabs were far worse. From behind the plazzglass, Farah began to weep, but her resolve did not falter. She would not let the monsters pass, not without taking out as many as she could. Kensei wanted to tell her to run, to go hide and let the crabs through, but how would that matter? If the crabs ate the sludge then the people or the people then the sludge, either way, once they'd finished with one resource they'd move on to the next. Terrifying as it was, Farah and everyone else trapped inside the Fortress needed to stay right here, so that if Kensei's plan worked, they'd be able to escape as soon as possible. Not having electronic communication was a serious inconvenience. Kensei hadn't even known where inside the hulking Fortress Farah had been. It gave him strength knowing she'd watch.

Thunder struck overhead, perhaps triggered by the newfound energy of the crabs, and it began to rain in earnest. Perfect.

'Now!' Kensei said and stripped off his clothes. He stood there naked while the men behind him balked. Only Roman followed suit, stripping naked and grinning next to Kensei, his brawny arms and hairy chest a reminder of the kind of man Kensei had always thought a woman as beautiful as Farah wanted.

'Here we go,' Kensei said to Roman and ran at the crabs. It was his life or hers, or worse of all, both. He could not let them take Farah from him, for then his life would be without meaning, his heart a discarded shell. It would be far easier to die for her.

The men grunted behind him as he and Roman ran into the mass of crabs and began hurling the creatures back into the open tanks of sludge. As Kensei had predicted, the diamondcrabs ignored them. The crabs began to eat the sludge spilled on the floor of the refinery from the great tanks. The men of Juxor, immigrants and native born, all equally desperate, seeing this, stripped down their clothes and charged at the wall of crabs trying to consume their Mothers of the Ocean. A hundred naked men threw the crabs over their shoulders.

'Don't hurt them!' Kensei said, reminding the men of his earlier hypothesis. The diamondcrabs could not perceive the men as food or as a threat. The rain, and lack of carbon-rich clothes should help with the food, and hopefully some sort of communal intelligence would take over and the crabs would realize that a far easier food source lay behind them, instead of in the tough walls of the Fortress that protected the women, children, and men cowering behind them.

They worked this way for hours in the rain. The naked, muscled men grabbed crabs and hurled them inside the factory, all while pipes dumped more and more of sludge on the floor. It seemed that despite their bravery, nothing would happen, for the waves of diamondcrabs were relentless. The women inside waited so long for their captors to free them that their distress changed to guarded optimism. They cheered as the men came closer and tore the crabs from the plazzglass, their claws clacking emptily instead of cutting through the substance, but eventually even their excitement gave way to exhaustion. There were just so many of the diamondcrabs, that no matter how many the men threw into the sludge, more rose from the sea and clambered onto the Fortress. Kensei would not stop, would not hesitate, and yet he began to wonder if his plan made any sense. He did not know how many of the hybrids there were. If they could not get a sizeable percentage of the population interested in an easier source of food, then all they'd succeeded in doing was feeding them. This entire plan hinged on the first holo he'd seen of the crabs, when a single individual had changed its behavior, signaled the others, and they'd listened. It was a behavior Kensei had never seen in a crustacean, yet his entire plan rested on the diamondcrabs communicating in such a way. It wasn't. The men were getting tired. Kensei's hands were raw, his back ached from being stooped for so long. His feet were bloody from the crabs climbing over him. He should be thankful for his life, thankful that the crabs hadn't turned on him, but part of him wished they would, at least then maybe it would give Farah a chance to escape. This went on for hours.

Then, after what felt an eternity, something changed. One of the crabs eating the sludge inside the refinery stopped and waved its claw in the air slowly. Another dozen copied, then a hundred more, then every diamondcrab on the Fortress was gyrating its little pincer to some unheard beat. The crabs abandoned their work on the Fortress and made for the factory like some horrid, clacking tidal wave. They devoured the sludge on the floor and began to spin their webs, filling the inside of the place with their black webbing. Some of them nestled down to change inside of the mass of fibers, others tended to those resting inside.

'Now!' Kensei cried out and scaled the ladder of the factory to the roof as other men slammed the metal doors shut behind the last of the crabs. It was inconceivable to assume they had captured all of the crabs, but that was not Kensei's plan. He hoped, when all this was through, he'd be able to help Juxor rebuild what they'd lost to the diamondcrabs.

Roman followed him, paying no heed to the man's asscrack in front of him, laughing ridiculously in the rain.

'Farah's gonna love this, Ikamon! You dog! I can't wait for the grand finale!'

They scaled the factory and when they got to the roof they found the fishermen waiting there, naked as they were when they came into the world, grinning like fools.

'Are we ready?' Ikamon shouted over the thunderhead.

'Ready sir!' they shouted back. Their nets had been spread over the windows. Dr. Fisk had asked why they were doing this and not just leaving the plazzglass in place, but Kensei had reiterated the importance of airflow. The doctor hadn't argued further, but he'd also refused to get naked and wait on top of the factory with the fishermen.

'Then get down from here, let's do it!' Roman said.

The men all clambered down ropes and ladders, burning their naked thighs on the rope, laughing like school children. Only one man had died, the guy who didn't follow the plan. From Kensei's vantage point atop the refinery he could see that the majority of the crabs had made it into the brick building. It was working! All they needed now was to light the fuse!

'Bow to me, priest of the Carbon Man.'

'Shit,' Ikamon cursed.

Kane approached the factory, wearing his rain slicker emblazoned with the carbon molecule.

'Come to me, creatures. Embrace me. Together, the Carbon Man and his Heralds will rule this world!' Kane said.

133

He grabbed the doors of the refinery that the fishermen had just closed and threw them open. Kensei watched through the window at the top of the refinery as Kane walked into the refinery through the hordes of creatures devouring every ounce of sludge. He extended his arms and the creatures swarmed over him, picking at his leather robes with the carbon symbol. A few crabs found his exposed hands. One snipped off a finger, but Kane didn't even call out. Instead he pointed to the Fortress. The crabs' eyestalks swiveled and looked at the fishermen between them and the women and children stuck in the Fortress. The diamondcrabs definitely had some sort of group intelligence, and Kane had just redirected their collective mind back towards eating people. Worst of all was that Kane wasn't dead, not yet. He began to walk back out of the refinery, bearing the crabs upon his shoulders. He was leading them back towards the Fortress.

'Now!' Kensei said, but the fuse wouldn't work. The flare popped to life, but it was attached to the inside of the door which now hung open. Kane had killed them all.

'I got it!' Osha McKenna yelled from down below. She was also stark naked, holding only a flare gun. Ikamon wasn't in the least bit surprised he'd missed seeing her, Farah was nearby, after all, but Roman's jaw hung agape, his flaccid penis rapidly growing.

'You know my favorite thing about carbon, Kane?' Osha asked as Kane tried to escape the crabs that burdened him. He couldn't go fast, the crabs had difficulty getting through his leather cloak, but their weight made it impossible for him to run. 'It burns.'

Osha McKenna fired the flare gun into the building. It found the sludge the crabs were consuming and lit up. In moments, the entire refinery was on fire. Great gouts of flame danced through the windows at the top of the building. Diamondcrabs struggled against the nets placed over the windows, but could not get through.

The crabs tried to escape from the front of the building, but the flow was too strong. A gale of force sucked the crabs into the blazes. They escaped the roof as smoke.

The factory burned for three hours before it ran out of fuel.

All that remained were the strands of webbing—far stronger than fire—and the creature's shells.

Kensei went to one, pulled it from its place in the webbing and cracked it open. He inhaled deeply, probing the flesh of the deadly creature. He put it to his tongue. It was good.

He approached the Fortress. A plazzglass panel, no longer held in place because of the diamondcrabs' furious appetite, fell away. To think, a moment later and the creatures would have been inside the Fortress, and Kensei's plan would have failed. Farah climbed over the sill, landed on the plazzglass, and slid down it, managing to keep her balance despite wearing a dress.

'Crab, for my Mango.'

'You fucking idiot I can't believe you would ever do something so stupid! You could have been killed!' Farah said, stomping through the mud and ignoring the light drizzle.

'If I had not risked my life, you would have surely lost yours. I cannot live without you, my Mango. You are not why I left my disgraceful family on Earth-1, but you are why I travel the stars. Please forgive me. *Gomenasai,*' Kensei said, bowing and extending the crab meat to Farah.

'That is some wannabe selfless bullshit. You think I would be happy if I had watched my dumb husband get eaten by bugs?' Farah snatched the crab from him. She took a bite.

Kensei waited, not daring to look up at her face. He stayed bowed, waiting, hoping, praying to his grandmother that Farah would take him back until he heard the sweetest sound in all of the inhabited worlds. Farah laughed.

'It's overcooked. But you know, my favorite part of our little meals was never the food,' Farah said.

'Oh?' Kensei said, standing up.

'It was the dessert.' Farah kissed Kensei, grabbed his naked ass, and pulled him to her.

The Mothers of the Ocean slowly emerged from their Fortress, climbing over the open window frame and sliding down the piece of plazzglass with trepidation. They tentatively smiled at the naked men standing around. No one's smile was bigger than Farah's.

'I can't believe you risked your life for me! That was so courageously dumb.'

Kensei smiled. 'Of course I would risk my life for you. I may be a dog, but I am still loyal.'

Farah sighed. 'Ken, for someone so smart, you can be a real moron.'

'I—forgive me,' Kensei bowed.

'Oh Darwin, get up. Look, you weren't ever supposed to hear that conversation. It was just girl-talk. Sometimes I feel that way about you, but didn't you hear what else I said? I'm thankful to have someone like you to spend my time with. I love the meals you make, and I must admit, a life-saving, roast crab feast is impressive.' Farah smiled. 'It's pretty amazing.'

'So you don't want to stay here?'

Farah turned and looked back at the other women and children. She shrugged. 'I don't know, Ken, maybe I do.'

'I understand,' Ken said, pushing away and trying to bow deeply to her.

'With you!' Farah groaned. 'I don't know, I've never really thought about it, but maybe it would be good to have a child one day. This planet could certainly use a fresh perspective, and hey, there's an opening for a marine biologist.'

Kensei could not find the humor in that.

'I don't think I want to get pregnant right now or anything like that, but maybe we'd make more of a difference here, and what they're doing is remarkable. They have art here, and sciences. I've never seen such culture anywhere except the Earths. I think we could be happy here. I'd be a goddess, and you'd be the planet's marine biologist... there are worse lives.'

Kensei nodded, happy his Mango wasn't mad at him, but shocked she'd consider leaving the *Artemis*. He'd do it in heartbeat for her, though. Much as he loved traveling, he loved Farah far more, and if this was where she wanted to have children, so be it. But all that could wait. All that mattered right now was that he had her in his arms, and if he let her go everyone from Juxor would see his erection.

20

'That was very impressive, Romeo. Was that how you imagined it would transpire?'

'Not at all,' Jupiter said, grinning. Osha and some of the men had gotten dressed; Jupiter made no such attempt. Osha shoved a slicker into his arms.

'I guess that's not the end of those creatures, though?' Osha said.

'No, it'd be virtually impossible to destroy them all, but Ikamon thinks you should be able to use this method to harvest them and keep the population down. Their shells can be used as industrial diamonds and the webbing survived the fire... I wonder if it could be used to make a new skylift cable,' Roman said.

'An interesting proposition. Considering only a few kilometers need replaced, it might be worth the risk,' Osha said.

'Osha, darling, tell me, who is your new friend?' Iris said, approaching her sister.

'This is Roman Jupiter. He was instrumental in helping stop the hybrids.'

Iris raised her eyebrows at Roman's naked body, making no attempt to hide where she was looking.

'I must say, you are an exquisite specimen. Good musculature, remarkably intelligent, and capable of making my sister call the crabs something besides aliens? Your genetics would make a fine addition to our work here.'

'I can't believe you're doing this!' Osha hissed.

'Oh, come now, you've made it quite clear you're not interested in him. He just risked his life for us and is standing here naked and you pay him no heed. Can't you see how hard he's working to control his poor penis? There's no need for that, Mr. Jupiter. Come, I'm due for another child, as are many of the other Mothers,' Iris said. Her eyes did not leave Roman's body.

A harem of a half dozen women approached. They had been mingling with the men who'd all risked their naked lives, but now the group of women approached Roman. Some had come at Ikamon, but Relkor had batted them away with profanity and threats.

'The Mothers have spoken,' Iris announced. 'Many of you risked your lives for us, and many of you will be rewarded,' she said to the naked men. 'No longer will we hide in our Fortress. From this day on there will be a feast every full moon. Those men that risk their lives against these hybrids will dine with us, those who are brave and agile will accompany us to the feast. Many of you will join us this night, but among the bravest and most clever were the two men of the *Artemis*. Though we don't practice it we will respect his monogamy, but the other,' she reached out an arm and stroked Jupiter's shoulder, 'the other will tell you all how it feels to be loved by the Mothers of the Ocean. Our time of secrets is past. The Carbon Man would be nothing without the Mothers of the Ocean, and Mothers are but a sea to be filled by the Carbon Man.'

Osha gritted her teeth. This was so typical. Any time she showed an interest in anything, her sister had to come in and swoop it up. And just when Roman was starting to get interesting.

'I couldn't possibly,' Roman said.

Iris smiled and moved her hand down his back, 'Oh it appears that you could.'

'Are, you, SERIOUS?' All eyes snapped to Farah Relkor, standing with Ikamon's arms wrapped around her.

'You really think *Roman Jupiter* is a good choice for a breeding partner? I can't believe I was actually thinking about staying here! You're all more foolish than I thought! I guess it makes sense. All you do is screw and keep the kids, huh? Roman should be great at that! Just make sure you don't turn off the lights halfway through or he might forget who he's in love with!'

'That never actually happened,' Roman mumbled to Osha.

'Come on, Ken. Let's get the hell out of here and go where we can bang in peace without a bunch of these Mothers trying to steal your seed.' Farah slapped her badge, hidden in her dress and smiled when Catalina responded. 'First Officer Relkor reporting for duty, Captain. I apologize for the lapse in judgement.'

The *Arrows* swooped over and landed on the far shore. Catalina stepped off and marched towards the crowd of naked men and scantily dressed women. It seemed they'd all tried to dress down to match the men.

'Officer Relkor. Glad to have you back. You are under probation for deserting your ship and have been demoted for your actions. Never forget that we serve the Charter.'

'But Captain!'

'Enough. Second Officer Ikamon, present yourself.'

Ikamon stepped forward and quickly brought his hands up to cover himself.

'Due to your actions and long service to the Institute, I, Catalina Solaris Xao Mondragon, captain of the O-class ship the *Artemis*, hereby promote you to first officer.

You're a damn good Biologist Mr. Mizuyama, my ship could really use a level-headed first mate,' she said, glaring at Farah. 'What do you say?'

Ikamon looked from Catalina to Farah, who, upon seeing Ken, erased the scowl from her face. 'Do it, Ken. Besides, I've always been turned on by men in power.'

'*Hai!*' Kensei bowed to his captain. 'I only have one question. Do you have to call me Mizuyama?'

'We leave at dawn, Ikamon,' Captain Mondragon said with a wink then turned and addressed the assembled people of Juxor.

'The Institute is sending a new marine biologist. We've informed them of the... ritual harvest. Awaiting confirmation, but if you all agree that harvesting the crabs for their shells and meat will work, I see no reason they'll object.'

'Here that, Roman?' Iris said to Roman. 'We have all night.'

21

Osha marched off through the crowd of women. Some of them were already leading men away, but many stood around waiting to see what would happen with their big catch. They weren't any better than the disgusting diamondcrabs, all hoping to what, *boink* Roman at once? Like human biology could even permit more than one or maybe two of them to be pregnant! Fools! Osha did not know why she was so mad. She didn't like Roman. His poetry was shallow, his motivations animalistic. What few men she was attracted to didn't have so much back hair. She couldn't care less about his obsession with fireflies, or his absurd belief in a firefly goddess. And she didn't like that he could think such things and still not believe in aliens. All in all, she had no reason to feel as awful as she did, and yet it hurt just the same to see her sister steal the handsome idiot away from her.

Osha stomped through the halls of the Fortress to her room. She grabbed a bag and began stuffing it with what she'd need if she wanted to survive out there. She didn't know where she would go, but she couldn't stay here anymore. Now, the only problem she'd ever helped solve had been incorporated into her sister's damn religion, and the man who'd help think of it would become their prized breeder. It was just too much. Osha grabbed her tablet and saw a yellowed note flutter to the floor. She knew right away it was another of Roman's damn poems, but she couldn't help herself. She picked it up and began to read.

A flame caught in a summer breeze
floating, flitting, fluttering, flying
alights upon five points of perfection
sucking, sipping, tasting, dipping.
She drinks her fill,
satiated in knowledge inextricable from the blood that flows in her hollow body.

She is wise,
wiser than me.
Knows her roots, knows which flowers to trust,
and which are but weeds.
To coerce this beauty into flight,
to see that brilliant orange dappled with spots,
to see that delicate proboscis,
tongue and lips' more sensual rival,
Do anything but what she wishes
is not my wish
wish it as I do

Osha looked up from the poem, tears in her eyes, to see Roman standing in the door frame. She sniffed, willing the tears not to fall.

'I... I don't get the reference.'

Roman smirked. He was dressed again, thank the Mothers, in his uniform for the Institute. He looked good like this, with his hairy chest peeking out of the zipper and his burly arms coming out of his rolled-up sleeves, but Osha had to admit, he looked better naked. The peeks of skin only hinted at the rest of his body. His package and muscular glutes were hidden beneath the jumpsuit. Osha found that after having seen him naked, it was hard not think of him that way. She found herself wondering if he was thinking the same thing about her. When she'd taken off her clothes and fired the flare she hadn't been thinking about Roman, though he was the first person to pop into her mind after the diamondcrabs had been neutralized.

'Sorry, I forget you've never left this planet. Seems amazing that someone so smart has never seen a monarch butterfly. They're beautiful. Orange the color of your hair and spotted with freckles on their wings just like you. They possess this amazing knowledge. Despite only living a few months — this is on Earth-1, of course — before they went extinct, they undertook a migration that took generations. A mother would leave her home in the mountains of a place called Mexico, lay eggs in Texas, the country that founded the planet, then that one would travel onward and lay eggs even farther north, and again once more until the fourth generation, then, sensing a change in the weather, would head all the way back to Mexico, making a journey that took its ancestors three generations to make.'

'That's very interesting,' Osha said.

'I think so too. I guess I just wanted to say once more how amazing you are, how you seem to have knowledge as powerful as their migrations. And, of course, like the monarch, your vibrant orange color is breathtakingly gorgeous.'

'Do male monarchs breed with whoever they wish?' Osha said, trying and failing to keep the emotion out of her voice.

'I told your sister that the only person on this planet I wanted to breed with was you,' Roman grinned.

'I should throw you through the Portal for that.'

'But?'

Osha rolled her eyes. 'But I enjoyed your poem immensely. I still don't quite understand your obsession with insects, but I do prefer being compared to a butterfly instead of a cannibalistic praying mantis.'

'That was only to show you my devotion!'

'It's still an unpleasant and flawed metaphor. I thank you for all that you've done. And it's OK if you want to breed with my sister and her friends. They're right, you have good stock. And I'm sure you'd make their time enjoyable.'

'Must I tell you the same thing I told that crowd of naked women?'

Osha looked up from her things. 'And what's that?'

'That there is only one woman on this planet with whom I wish to do anything resembling breeding, and she, possibly for the first time in my life, has resisted my charms. To have anything but you on this world would be akin to mistaking a fritillary butterfly for the noble monarch. Pleasurable, certainly, and not without its own beauty, but ultimately nothing but cheap mimicry.'

'You said all of that?'

'I told them that if I cannot have you, my place is in the stars on the *Artemis.*'

Osha nodded. Something about it sounded right.

'Besides, your insect population here is noticeably lacking, and the captain put in good word for me. If you're truly not interested, I guess I'll head back up to space.'

'So what, is this goodbye?'

Roman nodded. 'Do you wish to create a memory we can always cherish?'

'We are not going to copulate just because you're feeling sad.'

'Then this is goodbye.' Roman wiped a tear and smiled, then turned and left Osha in her room, alone.

22

Catalina was relieved that she'd elected to use the *Arrows* to get down to the surface of Juxor instead of the skylift. She'd made the decision to save time instead of fuel, and it had been a good choice, seeing as how the skylift no longer existed.

Catalina left the Bubblephone and made way for the *Arrow*. She found her crew waiting for her. How proud of them she was. Farah and Kensei, it seemed, had rekindled their romance, while Roman had for once been unsuccessful in his. Catalina had not exactly been pleased that they had come up with a ritual harvest to defeat the crabs that involved the men of the world stripping naked, but her superiors at the Institute didn't seem as skeptical. They'd praised Catalina and her crew for finding a new way to continue carbon production. Catalina couldn't argue with that. A few of the diamondcrabs had survived the fire, and rather than letting them emerge from their shells, Roman had suggested feeding them and harvesting the threads they produced like silk. Preliminary tests were already showing that the silk from the moth-dragonfly hybrids was far stronger than the material their factories had manufactured to create the tether for the space elevators. Osha had already written up a plan for how to join the threads. It would take a few weeks of testing, but seeing as the space elevator was broken anyway, the diamondcrabs' thread looked to be quicker and stronger than manufacturing more filaments. Soon, Juxor would have a space elevator made from the same creatures that had destroyed their last one. The usefulness of the creatures went beyond that, though. Kensei had proven they were delicious, and preliminary results showed they were fairly nutritious as well. One if the sludge-miners had recommended grinding up the shells to sell as rough diamonds typically used for polishing materials, processors or even batteries.

Yes, it seemed the *Artemis* had not only saved the lives of Juxor, but also reinvigorated their economy into some previously never-before-seen biological system. It sounded to Catalina like some ancient method of farming from earth. She should be proud. They'd awarded her another badge for saving Juxor's economy, approved her promotion of Ikamon, and given Roman his first badge for figuring out what the creatures were. So then why did Catalina feel so strange?

They'd solved Juxor's problem with the diamondcrabs and invented a strange new economy, but they'd also reinforced a corrupt, gendered religion. They hadn't removed the threat of the hybrids completely, and without careful management the problem would arise again. The marine biologist of the planet had died, as had over a dozen workers over the past few weeks, and yet the Institute had nothing but praise for the crew of the *Artemis*. It was bittersweet. Catalina had signed up for the Institute because she believed in the Charter, and had come to this planet because she believed the spirit of the Charter demanded she help save lives. She'd done it, and yet now it seemed the Institute was far more interested in the economy of the world. She supposed it was important to the region, but hydrocarbons weren't really *that* rare. Was Juxor that special?

Catalina couldn't know for sure. All she knew was that her crew was ready to take off, Fin was probably dying from boredom back on the *Artemis,* and this mission had brought them closer to Epsilon-V and investigating the creatures that had killed their last entomologist.

Catalina arrived at the *Arrow* to find her crew waiting.

'We grow for the Charter,' she greeted them.

'The Charter grows because of us,' they said back and Catalina smiled. Whatever else the Institute was doing, she was proud that it supported their work, and she was proud to work with these men and women.

'What's the plan, Captain?' Farah asked, hanging on to Ikamon.

'Onward to Epsilon-V. The institute has given us full discretion to do as we wish.'

'Hmm, strange, no? You'd think they'd give us a direct order to go to Epsilon-V if there are no more pressing concerns. Now that we have an entomologist with us.'

'You're being paranoid—wait I'm sorry. You're being paranoid, *sir!*' Farah said to Ikamon, but Catalina didn't think Farah really believed that Kensei was being paranoid, or at least not excessively so. No doubt about it, something was up.

'I have badges. Ikamon, present yourself.' Ikamon saluted and marched forward. 'For seeing the value of already established biological systems, I award you this badge of merit.'

'Thank you, Captain.' Ikamon bowed and accepted the centimeter-wide printed pin with careful grace and placed it next to his first officer badge of rank.

'Jupiter, present yourself.'

Roman grinned and marched up to Catalina. 'Captain, would it be possible to break tradition and have a civilian present me the badge?'

Catalina stopped herself. 'Yes, of course,' she clenched her teeth. A week ago, back in space, Roman had been drooling at the prospect of Catalina even touching *his clothes*, now he didn't want her to bestow him with a badge of honor? He could be so frustrating. 'Was there someone you had in mind?'

'Osha McKenna is coming this way, sir, perhaps it would be appropriate if she did the honors?'

Catalina turned to see that, indeed, Osha McKenna was approaching them, a large, wheeled suitcase in tow.

'Dr. McKenna, to what do we owe your presence?' Catalina asked.

'I would like to request passage off-world,' Osha said.

Everyone was speechless. Finally Ikamon managed to say, 'Really?'

'The reconstruction processes are proceeding well. My sister has accepted more of the men into the Fortress. They are laboring with our women to redesign and rebuild the skylift and to manage the hybrids. I am now, err...superfluous. All they want to do is work together and then talk about having kids and procreating. It's too much.'

'The *Artemis* is not an interplanetary transport vessel. Can't you charter something else?'

'Not with the skylift damaged. I expect it's going to be weeks before we even test the new tether. I'd appreciate an opportunity to travel with you at least to the next planet. Start a migration,' Osha said, her eyes finding Roman.

'Sir, Institute by-laws say that in times of emergency, we can carry passengers,' Farah said. 'Besides, she's smart as a whip, maybe we can get her to enlist.'

149

'She would be a strong addition to the Institute, sir, and our crew,' Ikamon said.

Catalina turned to Roman, surely the culprit behind this. His grin was cracking at the seams. 'What is your opinion, Jupiter? You've spent the most time with the doctor.'

'Sir!' Roman barked, his voice cracking, 'I do not think it would be a good idea to bring the doctor.'

'Oh?' Catalina said, all eyes turning to Roman, no one more shocked, it seemed, than McKenna. 'And why is that?'

'I think it would be better to tell you in private, sir?' Roman said. Then, more quietly, 'please, Sola?'

'Very well. A moment,' she said to the crew and marched a few meters away with Roman.

'I thought you were in love with her! Why on Earth-1 do you want to leave her here? Farah and Ikamon are right, she's smart and capable, and we certainly have room for a crew member, and she did enough to help you earn your badge.'

'It's *because* I love her, Sola. I... I've never met someone I love like her. She's beautiful and brilliant and passionate. Seeing her battle the diamondcrabs naked armed only with a flare gun made me fall deeper in love. I can't just forget about all that.'

Catalina clenched her jaw and tried not to tell herself that all of these things were true about their history, too, well, except for the flare gun part. It seemed she was a dim candle compared to Osha McKenna.

'Captain, if she comes with us and continues to rebuke me, as she's made it very clear she's going to do, it'll destroy me. You know I've always followed my heart. How am I supposed to function if it's broken?'

'Like the rest of us,' Catalina said and turned away from her ensign.

'Osha McKenna, we would be happy to escort you to our next destination, but I fear it is a mission fraught with peril. We could not leave you there, nor could we tarry or detour for your safety. If you wish to leave this world, I understand. All of us have felt the pull of the cosmos, or else we wouldn't be spacers, but I cannot grant you passage.'

Osha nodded, crestfallen.

'However, if you agree to come aboard in an advisory role we could pay you for your time. I would require you to take some prerequisite spacing classes and learn a bit about the Institute, as you'll be with us a while. You would not be required to go to the surface of Epsilon-V, but you would have to follow orders and be willing to give your life for this crew. Is that understood?'

'I only have one question.'

'Yes?'

'Do you have ovens? Can I bring my sourdough starter?'

'Mmm…I would have thought a poet and a chemist would know how to count,' Ikamon said, but he was smiling.

'Excuse me?' Osha said.

'You asked two questions, but the answer to both is the same,' Catalina smiled.

'Shit, you should have led with that. We'd take you without being a doctor if we'd known you could bake,' Farah said.

23

Try as she might, she could not resist him.

Though she found his actions on Juxor churlish, once on the *Artemis* it took but a day of his doting to sway her heart.

He came to her in her quarters. She was undressing, and didn't know why she answered the door clothed in nothing but a robe. His eyes, predatory and hunting, saw her plunging neckline and he pushed into the room with a grin. Already he was hard. Good. She was wet beyond comprehension.

He took her in the living room. They made loud, passionate love and screamed each other's names without bashfulness or thought to the crew. The *Artemis* was big enough, if someone didn't want to hear, they could go sit amongst the crickets.

24

'Oh, my Mango!'

'Ken!'

From her quarters, Osha McKenna could hear the married couple's labored grunts. She wished it was her having sex with Roman instead of the old married couple. At first, it hadn't been so bad. She found herself fantasizing about Roman and her having sex like that: loud, passionate, carefree sex. Osha had never really been interested in men. Her studies had always preoccupied her time. However, as she sat in her room, reading sonnets and listening to the married couple make love, she found her mind drifting to Roman's naked body again and again. But after two days of the noise, Osha finally gave up, put down the sonnets, and marched through the access tunnel in Ken and Farah's *Arrow* and into the main bulk of the *Artemis*.

'Is this typical behavior?' Osha McKenna asked Captain Mondragon when they reached the bridge.

'No,' Captain Mondragon said 'Normally they're a bit more discreet, but I don't have the heart to tell them to stop. If you want to stay up here instead of in an *Arrow* that might be better.'

'So there *is* some romance left in the old captain?' Roman said.

Catalina rolled her eyes. 'Ensign, just because you have a badge now does not mean your probation is over. Get cleaning.'

Jupiter went about the cafeteria, tidying up.

'I'm sorry you were down there. Why didn't you come up sooner?' Captain Mondragon said.

Osha nodded at Roman—who was pretending to wipe down a table but was staring at her from across the room.

'I… I was concerned about him.'

'Don't be. He can't lay a finger on you. He may be a horny scoundrel, but he respects women. He'd never be aggressive with you, and even if he was, just yell for help, the ship's comms are wired so I'd hear it. We'd all be there in a second and he'd be jettisoned into the abyss of space. Our Portal's not as gentle as the one back on your world.'

'No, it's not that.'

'Oh? Then what is it?'

'I know he asked to leave me behind, that he was worried that he'd continue to feel passionately about me and I would not reciprocate the feelings.'

'I wouldn't worry about that.'

'Ms. Mondragon, err *Captain* Mondragon, I uh, well… you two used to date?'

Catalina nodded.

'Well, look, has he ever given you anything like this?'

Osha passed Catalina a letter written in Roman's familiar script.

Dearest Osha,

I see now you are not a fan of poetry, so I must bare my heart in plain English. I love you. I love your cleverness, I love your passion to learn more, I love that you escaped a system run by your own family to chase your dreams. I find your hair and figure intoxicating, and wish that I could go back in time and see you fire that flare gun again, for in that moment there was never a woman more powerful or beautiful than you. And yet part of me fears that, because I will never be able to forget that moment where you saved your planet, I will forever pursue you. Like the lunar moth driven by the moon yet lacking a mouth, I will starve in my quest.

I wish you to be my moon, Osha. I wish you to be my nectar. I wish that when I go to sleep in my quarters you are there, forever, warming the bed or throwing away the sheets because your breath is hot from our throes of passion. If this is not a future you wish, then tell me, and I will come to terms with it and leave you be. But I beg you to think once more about what we could have. I will give you my everything. Like the black widow, I offer my life to you. It is yours to do with as you wish, for to be with you, I will die happy, and without you, I will simply die.

Yours, I hope, Roman.

Catalina took a deep breath, careful not to let her emotions show. Her time with Roman was passed. He'd written her his share of love notes, made his clunky metaphors about flowers and insects. That was behind them, where it belonged.

'What do you want me to tell you?' Catalina asked, but she saw it in Osha's eyes. The girl was heart-struck.

'I, well, I mean you dated him, correct? I have never done such a thing. On Juxor, sexual relations are exclusively about reproducing. And that never interested me. No one there has ever paid me this much attention. And I must admit, he *is* handsome.'

'Not a bad lover either,' the captain said.

'Oh,' Osha blushed. 'I guess. It's funny. I know I'm not going to be with you all for long, but maybe I should err… perhaps it is time that I try to… I mean, what's the worst that could happen?'

'You'll watch his love for your change to another woman. That passion, that way he looks at you, the way you know he's always thinking about you, all of that will evaporate as quickly as it came. If you're lucky it will only happen to you once, and you can forget all about it. I've watched him do it three times to me now, and it hurts a little less each time, but I don't think it will ever stop hurting knowing how single-mindedly he loves, and that that love was once mine.'

Osha nodded. She felt like a fool. She'd never felt *anything* like what Mondragon was describing. It sounded painful... but also powerful. Osha couldn't resist. She wondered if this was how drug addicts felt.

'Can I tell you a secret?' Osha said.

'Sure.'

'I'd never been with a man before, intimately, that is.'

'Never?' Catalina laughed.

'Shh! You said you'd keep it secret!'

'Sorry, wow. How old are you?'

'Old enough. I've just never come across an individual who seemed worthy of such a once in a lifetime event.'

'I can tell you this, Roman is definitely *not* the one. I can pretty much guarantee that the next planet we go to, he'll fall out of love with you and not so much as think about you unless maybe we go back to Juxor. He's a passionate lover, but a fickle man. He's not made for relationships.'

'Officer Relkor was already quite clear about his particular romantic eccentricities and I've taken them into account. I will not be here for too extended a period of time. So maybe, if it's OK with you, we can sort of date right now, and maybe, if it all goes well, Roman and I can well...'

'You want him to take your virginity?'

156

'No!' Osha blushed fiercely. 'Well...maybe. I just want to know if you think he'd be gentle with me, and understand that I've never, what do you spacers say? Boink?'

Mondragon laughed. 'If that's all you want, Roman is your guy. He's one hell of a lay, but can be as gentle as kitten too. He'll make you orgasm in ways that you... never mind. Yes, if that's all you want, then I say go for it. It bothered him when you came on because he thought he'd never have you, but maybe if you leave before he falls out of love, that'll finally set him straight.'

'So you think it'd be good?'

Catalina laughed. 'You're a diabolical little virgin.'

'Please, keep your voice down!'

'You're lucky you're not crew, or else I could bust you for giving a superior an order.'

'I am sorry, Captain.'

Catalina grinned. 'I'm just teasing you. Look, if you want my advice, I think you have a great couple weeks ahead of you. Roman is a fantastic lover. I can't think of anyone I'd rather be stuck in a bedroom with for a few weeks. You understand that he has duties to this ship, of course.'

'Captain Mondragon, please, it's not like I'm some sex-starved hussy!'

Catalina raised an eyebrow and Osha blushed ever more fiercely, her freckles disappearing in the red.

'You have my blessing. I think it's a great plan, and if you can make it happen before he falls out of love with you, all the better. Just be warned, if you fall for him, it hurts badly when you see all that love or lust or whatever the hell he feels move to another.'

Osha nodded.

'Well, if there's nothing else, Fin, take us into Bubbledrive.'

'Affirmative,' Fin said over the comm and, just for a moment, Osha wondered how much the pilot had heard. Probably all of it. Ah well.

Osha stood up, holding the letter in one hand, and approached Roman. She gently grabbed Roman by the shoulder.

He turned and smiled. Seeing it was her, he smiled larger.

'Osha, please, if you are to touch me that way I don't know how I can possibly control myself. I will do my best, of course, but perhaps you can wear something less revealing.'

Osha smiled. She was wearing a grey jumpsuit. The front was unzipped, but she had on a white t-shirt underneath. The idea of accepting Roman's love was palpable. If he was like that when she was clothed, how would he be when they were alone? It made her moist just thinking about it, imagining his hands or even his tongue bringing her to climax, his rough cheeks scraping against her thighs. It would all be hers soon!

'Roman. I read your letter. You're right. I want to try this. I don't know for how long, but I want to give it a shot.'

Roman's eyes smoldered, his grin grew even wider. 'Even if it's for a single kiss, I will treasure it always. You've been all I could think about. It's a wonder we were able to stop the diamondcrabs at all considering how much of my attention you consumed. Like the mayfly, I will rise from the waters to satiate your lust, like the sunflower, always turning to face you.'

'Mhmm...' Osha pressed herself against Roman. He got the hint, stopped talking, and moved to meet her lips. He smelled earthy and musky, the way a man was supposed to smell. One hand wrapped through her curly red hair and the other caught the small of her back and leaned her backwards ever so slightly, just enough for her to know he held her. He groaned softly in anticipation as their lips came together. His lips locked with hers, and for a moment their kiss was everything. She found her hands wrapping around his broad shoulders, mussing his hair, breathing him in. She felt his hard body press against her breasts, her body, her thighs. It was like melting into another being, her first kiss, first *real* kiss anyway, a moment of transcendence she'd only ever found in a textbook. She was not herself anymore, but something more. Something awakened inside of her.

She pulled away. Her eyes seeing Roman for the first time. He looked back at her with the same passion, that look that she was his universe, his everything. That all he wanted was her. She smiled. He grinned.

'Thank you,' he said and Osha swooned. It was she who should be thanking him!

'Bubbledrive in 3...2...1...'

Through the plazzglass windows of the *Artemis* the darkness of space flickered into an aurora of lights as the ship commenced stretching space to be able to arrive sooner than a beam of light. Roman's brown eyes sparkled under the dancing colors until they left her and drifted across the room.

'Roman?' Osha said and kissed him again, but his lips did not kiss her back.

'I'm sorry. I don't know what came over me. Excuse me.' He shook his head, as if to dislodge water from his ear.

He left her there, her clothing still warm from his body, her hair amess, her mouth half open waiting to finish another kiss. He slicked back his hair and straightened his uniform as he approached the captain.

'Captain Sola,' Osha heard Roman say. 'Your hair looks amazing in this light. Tell me, what are you doing this evening? Perhaps after dinner we could discuss the fireflies I found on Juxor? I also traded for some oysters if you're interested.'

Though she couldn't see his face, Osha knew that Roman was waggling his eyebrows, trying to impress Catalina.

Tears clouded her vision. The pain was immediate, the heartbreak entire.

'I'm sorry,' Captain Mondragon said, but Osha didn't want to hear it. The captain had warned her of this, though Osha had hoped to have more than a single kiss from the man to whom she'd sacrificed her heart. She ran from the bridge, past the labored grunts of Ikamon and Officer Relkor. She threw herself in her quarters on one of the *Arrows,* as far from Roman as possible. What had she done? She'd left her life behind, for what? For a man?'

No, Osha shook her head. She was doing the right thing. Leaving her sister was hard, leaving her home had been difficult, but she would weather the storm. She had only hoped that Roman would have been there to weather it with her.

End of Book 2

Acknowledgements

First off, with my deepest gratitude, I would like to thank Josiah Davis for editing this book. Your work makes this story so much stronger, and I am so sorry for the number of commas I have probably misplaced in this sentence alone. You were the first professional I've had work on a manuscript, and I could not be more pleased with what you've made this story become. A big hearty THANKS to everyone who read this book in its infancy. Tom Mitchell, thanks for taking the time. Brian Becker, your notes are much appreciated. I'd also like to thank everyone who jumped at the opportunity to get their hands on the first book. It's not easy gaining momentum on this self-publishing thing, but y'all are making it easier. So thanks, Dave, for texting me a pic of the paperback before I even got my copy. Thanks, Coach Howry, for getting one and sorry for still calling you Coach. Thanks, Amy, thanks, Jack, thanks, Carlos, and Minerva. Thanks to my mom, Zena Mitchell, for finding typos I needed to fix and also telling me not to worry about it (yeah right!). And last of all I'd like to thank my amazing wife, who has read too many versions of this story and heard far too many mumbled attempts as well. Raquel, darling, I could never do this without you. Thank you for letting me wake up and write while you let Leo nibble on your body in the pre-dawn light. You are amazingly caring and I will start on your breakfast soon, I promise.

ICEOAKS AND WARBLERS

Interstellar Spring Book 2

Available May 22nd 2017 on amazon.com

Until then enjoy this sneak preview! If you are interested in receiving an advance copy for review or for any questions, comments, publishing concerns, or anything else please visit

www.jdarrismitchell.com

'Space-pirates,' Ikamon said.

Everybody then started talking at once then.

'Are there reports in this sector?'

'Do you think they'll want my fireflies?'

'Surely you can dodge a ship at this speed.'

Fin answered only her captain. 'Yes, Captain, if it is a ship, of course I could dodge at this speed, and it's highly unlikely they could calculate our speed enough to drop into Bubble with us, and even if they did I could leave them behind with a little bit of maneuvering. The danger is that if it's meteoroids, or a broken-up ship or something like that, then the pieces will tear through us. Our sensors are telling me that there's mass, but can't tell me the exact dispersal, the bending of spacetime distorts all that.'

'So you think we should drop from Bubbledrive?'

'It's your call, Captain. If it is meteoroids, we should definitely drop from Bubble, if it's uh... saboteurs, then we shouldn't.'

Captain Mondragon nodded. Osha was confused— here the crew was debating whether it was a meteor field or space pirates, and they seemed to be more worried about the pirates!

'Statistically it has to be meteoroids. We had a lot of men come to our planet. No one ever got attacked in space,' Osha said. She'd only been aboard the *Artemis* a few weeks, and thought she couldn't regret it any more than she already did.

'They were probably all from the over-populated Earths. It's different the farther out you go. And right now we're between Hera's Hall and Ron's World. It's an area not patrolled by the Institute or the United Worlds,' Roman said. It was flabbergasting how clinical he was to her after how obsessive he'd been back on Juxor. He wore his uniform with the sleeves rolled up and the front zipper down just enough to show his hairy, muscly abdomen. Osha tried to keep her eyes off of him.

He went on, 'I vote we listen to Captain Sola. Her wisdom has never led us astray, and I might add that if it is space pirates surely her beauty would make them rethink any transgressions against us.' It became much easier for Osha to ignore the buffoon.

'There's no fruiting way it's pirates,' Farah said.

Osha was relieved someone agreed with her.

Ikamon shrugged. 'I've read reports from scouting vessels. Apparently they can be a real problem. They take cargoes of plants and fish eggs mostly, then sell them to the less-established worlds. People are hungry, you know?'

'That kind of thing never happened on Juxor!' Osha said.

'Are you sure about that?' Farah asked, 'I saw your greenhouses. Some of those plants aren't typically approved for Interstellar transport, not hardy enough.'

'Your supposition is that they were stolen?'

It was Farah's turn to shrug. 'Maybe, maybe not, but they were almost certainly smuggled. At the very least someone was bribed. Pirates do all that.'

'I can't believe this. Roman surely you don't believe all this?'

'I believe whatever Sola believes,' Roman said, grinning at his captain with love in his eyes.

Captain Mondragon hesitated hardly a moment. 'Fin, drop from Bubbledrive. I want everyone on high alert. Officer Relkor and Ikamon I want you on your levels; if they are after specimens that's where they'll go. McKenna, I want you to stay here with Fin, it's the safest place on the ship. Jupiter, do we have any red wasps?'

'Yes, Captain. I was thinking we have a moth that might do some damage, though of course wasps are a much better idea. You are so brilliant.'

'You have a job to do.'

'Yessir.' Roman followed the crew off the deck.

'I don't understand, you think there's a risk of being boarded, so you're having your crew go ready their animals?'

'Understand this, Doctor, the chances of us being boarded are tiny. We are a vessel of the Institute, who possess unthinkable sway and funds. Despite Ikamon's warnings, an Institute vessel has never been boarded. Most likely we will drop from Bubbledrive and find ourselves in an asteroid field. We will navigate it and try to ascertain its origin. Anomalies like this are unusual. Most gravitational masses on the paths between the inhabited worlds are very well documented. Otherwise the Bubbledrive paths wouldn't work. We need to figure out what has caused this.'

'So then why did you send your crew to go prep wasps?'

Fin turned and grinned. 'Every vessel prepares for this. The Institute is non-violent. Our ships don't have guns, and on top of that, we're always chock full of valuable terraforming organisms. We'd be the perfect hit. Every captain has a plan to protect their ship. We've been ready since before Doctor Mercurian died on Epsilon-V.'

'Chances are still slim anything will happen, but it is best to be prepared. Fin, what's our status?'

'The mass is approaching. I'll accelerate into it and then drop out.'

Captain Mondragon nodded.

Fin hit a few controls. For a moment, the aurora outside the ship flashed even more exuberantly, and then the un-bent view of space returned. One star hung in this distance, slightly brighter than the rest that filled the sky, scattered like diamonds on velvet. All around the ship were chunks of ice. In front of the *Artemis* was a single, hulking asteroid.

'There's our problem then?' Osha asked.

Fin ignored her. 'Captain, it's a type-B asteroid. Hardly moving at all relative to the background stars. Someone put it there.'

'And the debris?'

Fin typed a few commands into her console and one box of the screen expanded. There were tiny rocks all spread out. 'Mostly ice. I can pilot through them at this speed no problem, but under Bubble they would have riddled us with holes. Maybe someone dropped the asteroid here as a warning?'

'Possibly,' Captain Mondragon said, but for once she didn't sound sure of herself. 'Proceed, Fin. You're not getting any readings indicating anything else?'

'No, Captain, the asteroid is made of heavy metals, otherwise we might never have spotted any of this from Bubble. Other than that, the debris seem to be spread apart in a random pattern.'

'Let's go as quickly as we can.'

Fin nodded and nudged the *Artemis* forward. As it crept through, bits of ice gently bumped against the plazzglass windows that covered the front of the ship and careened off into space. They would twist forever in patterns defined by a chance encounter. Slowly, the *Artemis* moved through the field of ice, edging closer to the asteroid. It was a dark, shadowy thing—what little starlight there was did nothing to illuminate its cratered surface.

'Can't you go any faster?' Osha said.

Fin shook her head. 'There's too much debris and no real pattern to it. No holes to dodge through. It's going to be slow going for a while.'

'Osha, while we have a moment, I would like to talk about what's been happening.'

Osha sighed and tried not to blush. 'Captain, please, that won't be necessary,' Osha said, eyeing Fin.

'Fin, headphones?'

'You never have to ask me twice,' Fin said, pulling out a large pair of clunky headphones and putting them over her ears. After a moment, loud sounds that could maybe pass for music blared from them. Osha sighed. Fin was engaged in navigating through the field. Occasionally, larger chunks of ice would appear from the darkness. With a deft hand, Fin would twist and twirl the *Artemis* out of the path of these larger chunks, all the while knocking away the smaller pieces of ice and staying wide of the massive asteroid. She could not save Osha from the awkwardness that was to come.

'Dr. McKenna, I'm sorry that Roman fell back in love with me. I wish there was something I could do for you.'

'You've done quite enough as it is.'

'I never wanted this to happen. Since he's been back on my ship he's been strange. Every time we go to a planet he starts lusting after someone, which is what I had come to expect, but now it seems whenever he sees me under Bubbledrive he falls back in love with *me*. I don't know how else to explain it.'

'Wait.' Osha's mind raced. 'This happens every time you go to Bubbledrive?'

'Well, it's happened twice now, and when we used to date he was always most passionate under Bubble. He composed many a love song about my skin under the light of the auroras.'

'That is distinctly irregular, don't you think?' Osha said, something occurring to her.

'Roman is anything but regular.'

'Yes, but to fall in and out of love like that is unusual even for people who have my sister's lifestyle. And he talked about your skin? He talked about my skin when we were on Juxor. What if there's something wrong with him? It is possible that Bubbledrive affects his hormones!'

'Osha, I think you're reading into things. He's not worth your virginity. He's not worth much except as entomologist. It's probably best to ignore him until we get you to Guadalupe.'

'With your permission, sir, I think it's increasingly clear we're not under attack. If anything, this warning asteroid just proves how non-violent mankind has become. I would like to go see Roman, and ascertain if he's uh... any different?'

Mondragon sighed. 'I suppose so... just, don't get your hopes up, OK?'

'Yes, Captain Mondragon,' Osha said, but it was too late, she already had. She hit the elevator button and dropped down to the fifth floor, oblivious to the complete reversal of the artificial gravity on the elevator. It never ceased to amaze Osha how huge the *Artemis* was. While most ships were as big as a house, the *Artemis* was more like a factory. It had fifteen levels just for libraries of organisms, plus the top deck for the bridge, cafeteria, sleeping quarters and whatnot, and the bottom floor was a massive laboratory. Everywhere, the artificial gravity more or less pulled one towards the center of ship, except for the aft where all of the engineering systems were and where gravity was bit odd. Gravity didn't shift on the *Arrows*. The transport vessels turned living quarters were usually lined up in the front of the ship in a single shaft that stuck out from the huge, bow-shaped body of the

Artemis to keep the mass of ship in line with the stretching of the Bubbledrive, but either Mondragon or Fin had moved them. Instead of in one big line they dotted the front of the ship like spikes. Ostensibly, it was to minimize the surface area of the *Artemis* and thus make Fin's job of navigating the ice field easier, but it also served the dual purpose of providing an escape pod on every level. Osha rolled her eyes. How paranoid. She lived on a world beyond the Earths and they'd never heard tales of space pirates, and surely if any ships were to be raided it would have been the carbon-rich vessels leaving her home of Juxor. *Former home…*

Osha couldn't help but forget all that when she saw Roman. He was tending to a papery wasp's nest, and stood in front of a plazzglass window, his burly physique silhouetted against outer space. He looked amazing. His uniform's sleeves were still rolled up despite dealing with a mass of stinging insects. Behind him was a clear glimpse of the universe. The area the ship had gone through was a near-perfect circle that pointed to the stars behind them. The *Artemis* had cleared the ice in a path, framing Roman perfectly against the stars

'Roman!' Osha waved.

Roman grinned. 'And to what do I owe the honor of this visit?'

Osha smiled inwardly. This was more like it! Maybe the Bubbledrive did affect his hormones! He gently put the wasps back in the case and closed the plazzglass covering. 'It looks like we're going to be OK, huh?'

Osha nodded. 'Yeah, everything appears to be quiet.'

Roman nodded and turned to look behind him. 'Funny how beautiful it is. I wonder how long this asteroid field has been here, considering there's no paths through it except for ours. Lucky us, I guess.'

'Yes, lucky…' But it couldn't be luck. If someone had put in all the effort of moving that asteroid into the middle of the field of ice, surely there would be some sign of their passing, just as there were clear signs of where the *Artemis* had been.

'It's a trap!'

'You are in breach of the United Worlds' Treaty of Guadalupe. You are attempting to hijack the Artemis, a vessel of the Institute for Organic Expansion. We are a *protected craft.*'

'And what makes you so damn special?' a voice distorted to mask the identity of the speaker said back.

'We preserve life in the name of the Charter!' Catalina said resolutely.

The garbled voice only laughed in response.

'This is Fin Zerog, pilot of the Artemis. We don't have any cargo of real value, just tell us what you want and we can work something out.'

'We are not negotiating with these scoundrels. They have no right to anything aboard this ship,' Catalina said. Fin had never seen her captain so indignant, but no one had ever tried to rob the Institute before, so Fin supposed it was justified. That didn't mean the pirates would listen politely.

'Captain, they won't touch this ship if you don't want them to,' Fin said, grabbing the controls with a wicked grin.

'Sorry, Fiona, it's not that simple,' the garbled voice said.

'Who is this? How do you know that name?"

The voice laughed again. 'Haven't changed a bit. This won't take long. Just open a landing bay at on engineering. We'll get what we need and be on our way.'

Fin gripped the controls and began to rotate the Artemis in time with the smaller vessel coming from the asteroid. The little ship was faster than the hulking *Artemis,* but all Fin had to do was keep the front of the *Artemis* pointed at the pirates so they couldn't come around and go for engineering. Try as the pilot of the little ship did, they couldn't outmaneuver Fin. She twisted and gyrated the controls of the ship and it responded. The field of frozen meteors spiraled and spun through the plazzglass windows. Fin's skills were such that it almost seemed that, instead of keeping the pirate ship at bay, she was guiding it into pieces of ice, for it crashed and smashed into the meteors recklessly, sending them careening this way and that.

'Face it. You can't touch us. The debris field was a good ploy, but you're not getting to engineering.'

'We could have done this simply,' the garbled voice said and the little ship stopped dashing around the *Artemis.* Its jets flared and it rocketed towards the larger vessel. It was much faster than the other, larger ship it had come from.

'What are they doing?' Captain Mondragon said.

'I'm not sure. Even if they do manage to punch a hole in the *Artemis,* their ship will be destroyed,' Fin said.

'What's our choices, pilot?'

'Try to dodge,' Fin said as her fingers twitched over the controls. 'But that's probably what they want anyway, or let them hit us. They might knock out some plazzglass, but our sensors say that ship is mostly ultra-light alloys. They'll be obliterated. The specimens all have their own life support. Even if we need repairs we'll be fine once we're back under sunlight.'

'*Perfecto.*' Catalina said, grabbing the arms of her Captain's chair and gritting her teeth.

The ship drew closer to the *Artemis*, aiming for the front of the ship instead of the bridge. Fin was quite certain they'd pull away, until the front of the little speeder opened up like a flower and ejected a smaller, oblong object.

'What is that thing?' Captain Mondragon asked.

Fin didn't know. The object had no thrusters, yet was hurtling towards the *Artemis* at speeds far greater than the ship it came from. 'It's made of heavier stuff than the ship, Captain. It's going to puncture us!'

Fin tried to spin the *Artemis* up, but the projectile was too fast. It smashed into the 4th floor of the *Artemis* and alarms started to blare.

'Jupiter, they're coming your way.'

Made in the
USA
Lexington, KY